Discouraging at BEST

Also by John Edward Lawson

Novels

Last Burn in Hell (Picaresque Book One)

Collections

Pocket Full of Loose Razorblades

Poetry

The Troublesome Amputee

The Plague Factory

The Horrible

The Scars are Complimentary

As Editor

Tempting Disaster

Sick: An Anthology of Illness

Of Flesh and Hunger:Tales of the Ultimate Taboo

Discouraging at BEST

John Edward LAWSON

RAW DOG SCREAMING PRESS

With special thanks to
Kevin, Kristina, Dave, Shelby, Dennis, Jeanne, and Jennifer.

$ $ $

For the world, and its Kind Sirs in particular.

Published by Raw Dog Screaming Press
Hyattsville, MD

First printing 2007

Cover image: "The Trend Is Over" by Dennis Sibeijn,
www.damnengine.net
Book design: M. Garrow Bourke

Printed in the United States of America

ISBN: 1-933293-19-5 / 1-933293-33-0

Library of Congress Control Number: 2006928777

www.rawdogscreaming.com

Table of Contents

"...Left Behind in the Abstrusified Zone Designated as the United States of America"

by Kevin Dole 2

THERE ARE NO HAPPY families in *Discouraging at Best*. Nor healthy families, nor sane ones.

Leo Tolstoy's famous maxim about the misery of every unhappy family being unique is proven true once more, but *Discouraging at Best* is a book that can only be done justice by replacing the word "unhappy" with the phrase "batshit loony."

Whether black or white, rich or poor, each featured clan boils with the kind of dysfunction that goes nuclear when left unchecked. The Havenots rent themselves out as "disciplinarians" to their neighbors. The Pretorious clan brawls all night until their house is carpeted with blood and broken glass. These families are not so much dissected as allowed to tear themselves apart on the page. The reader gets to see inside and it isn't pretty.

One of these families lives inside the White House. The patriarch is the President of the United States. He is a dim man obsessed with sex and imagined supernatural forces. His administration is comprised of racist crooks. Aside from an addictive substance called "aqua aqua," it's not exactly unfamiliar.

This is why *Discouraging at Best* is so funny. It may never firmly establish itself as a loose novel or a tight collection of long stories but this ambiguity in no way impedes its hilarity. You'll cringe at times, your mouth will hang open, but you'll laugh a lot if you can accept it on its own terms.

This is a stream of conscious satire that constantly changes shape. Some segments steam forward with the intensity turned up to eleven while others float lazily around the banal before abruptly landing on the shocking. Both ways keep the pages turning and, no matter how much you think ahead as you turn them (and there is a great deal to think about) you'll rarely see what's coming next.

No matter what the form, it's usually political, if often slyly so. John Edward Lawson displays a deep suspicion of power that is only natural to one who has spent much of his adult life in close approximation to his nation's capital, but not in the overblown, obnoxious, and, above all, obvious manner that readers have come to expect from works about life in these United States. Instead he takes a note from Dr. James Dobson and keeps his focus of the family, where the heart is.

Dr. Lawson's prognosis? Re-read the title of this book.

And where does that leave us? Re-read the title of this essay—it's a quote from inside the book.

Discouraging at Best is a book I'm glad to have. It reminds me a bit too much about the world in which we live, but at least it helps me laugh about it.

—Kevin Dole 2
August, 2006

Whipped on the Face With a Length of Thorn Bush: Yes, Directly on the Face

"...AND OTHER PLACES, OTHER extremities of the body *if you will*," he added, wanting to make the whole deal sound as brainy as possible. "That's what you'll tell 'em boy, got it?"

"Yes sir." The response was reluctant, soft. Malcolm was only seven at the time, and not especially athletic. As it stood he was the only son the family could boast, curse him, so what else could they do? White folks weren't in this position, no, having to make the youngins go tromping all about in the interest of making money. If only Hershel were still with them...

"Come on now, whip that thing like I done showed you." With crossed arms he stood back and watched his son go at it with alacrity, working up his nerve with each stroke to part the air. "Good, good, could be better though."

This was his scheme of schemes; no way could this fail to bring home the bacon. They were caught in a summer break like any other, which is to say all these shiftless little freeloaders needed to be put to work. Yes, hmm, yes...the boy seemed to be getting the hang of it. After growing resentful, day in and day out, of seeing that four-foot length of thorn branch laying on top of the tool shed—well, what passed for a tool shed anyhow—July had finally put the wretched thing to use. This son of his would go from door to door, yes, with that supple, imposing thorn switch, and he would hawk his wares, oh yeah, unlimited whippings for just five bucks.

Just then the wife burst in on the scene, eyeballing the sugar bag which had been split open after a particularly vicious and poorly aimed fling of the thorns. "July! July, what in the world is all this commotion?" Without waiting for an answer Ernestine spat out, "Don't you have any sense in that head? The girls are asleep and here you are," she paused, flailing her arms aimlessly trying to imitate them in that god-awful pink muumuu, "thrashing the family belongings with that there stick! Don't got any sense between the two of you, man and boy."

As the man of the household July simply could not let this affront slide. "*We* are *working*. *You*, woman, are just standing around, taking up space, and blabbering like some kind of *signifying monkey!* Now get yourself gone and let us work."

"How dare you talk to me that way? Malcolm," Ernestine croaked, snapping her fingers at the confused boy, "go up to your room right this instant. Me and your father are going to have ourselves a *conversation*."

July wanted to smack those pursed lips right off her face but instead found himself saying, "Malcolm you aren't going anywhere, you're staying right where your father tells you to."

"*No*, you are *not* boy; you are marching right on up to that room of yours this instant!"

The befuddled boy looked back and forth between his embattled parents like a tennis spectator, his anxiety mounting, one gloved hand still nervously clutching the thorn branch. At the first indication of movement on Malcom's part July chimed in with, "Uh-uh-uh!"

With hands on hips Ernestine retorted: "*Oh uh-huh uh-huh uh-huh!* And leave that stick down here boy, what's wrong with your head?"

"He will do no such thing! If I tell to him to hold onto that he will—"

"Oh no he won't!"

"—and if I tell him to whip you with it then by God he will!"

"Oh!" Ernestine exclaimed. "Why don't you go on and slither around on your belly while you're at it! *And Malcolm you put that stick down this very instant!*" Certainly the girls had been awakened by now, but that was no longer the point.

"First of all, you ignoramus, that is not a *stick*, it is a *fibrous vine*, that means it's stiff and hard and bendy—"

"Oh, well, it's 'bendy' is it?!"

"Yes, it is! And second of all, Malcolm...whip your mother!"

"*He will do no such thing!* July you—"

"Oh yes he will! Oh yes he will! He's my son! Boy, you take that there length of thorn bush to your mother's hind side this instant!"

Repulsed by the scenario they had created for themselves Ernestine turned her wrathful glare to her son. "Malcolm Elijah Baxter, if you raise that stick to me I *swear*, *I swear*, on the grave of your grandmama, that I will disown you here and now!"

"Malcolm!" July cried, the ligaments in his neck threatening to spring loose. "What're you waiting for?! I'm gonna count to three and if you don't whip them thorns on your mama's flesh I will, and you *know* I mean it when I says it, I will whip them thorns on you!" Hershel would've whipped her...

"Don't you listen to him. I gave birth to you, he didn't," Ernestine stated in a last-ditch attempt at maintaining control.

"*One...*"

"July, you are turning into a white devil!"

"*Two...*"

Suddenly the boy let loose a startling scream, stress-induced tears squirting inches from his eyes as he shrieked horribly. Then, quaking almost to the point of convulsions, he fled the confines of the argument, of the house, taking the thorn branch with him as he ran.

Quietly cultivating a terrible rage July turned on his wife, his gloomy eyes wide and unmoving like a zombie. "Damn it woman, you up and turned our boy into a *sissy!*"

$ $ $

Malcolm lived in mortal terror of his father's seemingly random outbursts and, worse still, the threat of his mother's love being taken away from him, as it was the only comfort allowed him in life. He had witnessed his father punching holes in the living room wall in a fit of drunken enlightenment; he had watched, terrified, as his father bellowed epithets at the formless winds, louder by far than the apocalyptic booms of thunder overhead, for several hours, during which Malcolm had been chained to the big old green chair they used to have on the porch. The whole thing had ended with a bolt of lightning striking the only tree occupying their front yard, which in turn collapsed on the enclosed porch—well it was enclosed back then anyway—and fragments of fiberglass had embedded themselves in Malcom's arms and legs. Too frugal to permit a trip to the emergency room Malcom's father had growled "Take it like a man!" at the five-year-old. In the following months the infections failed to kill Malcolm entirely, instead leaving him grotesquely scarred. Most of the time it was okay, but when he ran or played games the remaining slivers of fiberglass would slice at his muscle tissues from the inside, tormenting him to no end.

He came to rest in one of the drainage ditches running through the neighborhood, struggling not to cry like a little girl, not to carry on like a pansy little sissy-boy. No, Malcolm hadn't a clue as to what a pansy was, but his father always managed to say it with such malice that he knew he could never allow himself to be seen as a pansy by others, not even when the internal bleeding in his arms and legs would cause dark pools to form under his skin.

After laying in the mud for close to an hour and a half he was able to get himself under control once more. Just as he was considering making a go of returning home a jet of yellow flew overhead, spattering against the opposing incline of the ditch. Lowdown—nasty old Lowdown—was standing above him, urinating what smelled like ammonia and rotting fish, blind drunk. This enraged Malcolm, he didn't know why, and what's more he didn't care. The gloves? They were still on his hands. His teeth? Gritted, gnashing, abusing themselves because of this damn drunk that everybody hated. The length of thorn bush? Yes, it was still in his grip.

With a maddened cry that scared even himself Malcolm swung the thorn branch, gripping it in both gloved hands, giving his entire body and last reserve of energy to the effort. Dutifully those hook-like points dug into the underside of the homeless man's penis, tearing along its underside, and just as quickly they exited. Having the course of its flow interrupted by a new opening the bloody urine sloppily found its way directly to Malcolm now in one thick gush. Above him Lowdown hollered for all he was worth, actually much more than he was worth, and awkwardly shambled away through the streets gripping the base of his savaged penis. "Go-damn, Go-damn, Go-damn th' boy done broke th' bone, Go-damn!" He continued on like this until he was either dead or simply out of Malcom's hearing.

With the drunkard's crimson stew soaking into his sweatshirt Malcolm collapsed in the mud, unconscious.

$ $ $

Quadira was afraid, yes, but not because of how her brother had been found in that filthy ditch. There had been those familiar pains in her stomach, just like the month before, and that evening after dinner she had noticed...blood.

"Oh God! Oh God!" her mother wailed, still frenzied in her sorrow, her remorse, her rage. "How could you do this! How could you do this to him! Our only son! Oh God!" she sobbed.

Quadira's parents had no clue about the sinister secret gnawing away at her, deep inside her...no, no! They could never be told. It was simply too horrible.

Her father sat in his favorite chair, implacable, reading the newspaper as he did every night on which no sports events were broadcast. "*Well?!*" Quadira's mother screamed at him. "*Aren't you going to say anything for yourself?!*"

After finishing the sentence he was reading Quadira's father replied, "Who? Oh, me? I thought you were talking to God." When he was this cold Quadira could plainly see his handsomeness shining through.

"Damn you, you worthless man, I am talking to you! Who else?! Who else but you drove our little boy out of the house with that insane bunch of yah-yah?! You tell me! You tell me!"

"If I remember correctly you're the one who came in hollerin' and carryin' on and all and upset the boy so."

It was the squirrel. Oh Lord help her, it was the squirrel again!

Standing over Malcom's drenched, stinking body like some kind of poor-man's tombstone Quadira's mother shook her fists at the man trying so hard to ignore her. "*Me?! Me! Quadira! Did you hear that?! Josephine! Did you hear that?! Me! Me!* Oh God hold me back, somebody hold me back!"

Since nobody was stepping in to hold his wife back Quadira's father added, "Plus on top of it all you're the one that made the boy a sissy to begin with. Running outta here screaming like a rat with its tail chopped off! He always was an embarrassment to the family."

Quadira wrapped her arms around herself, almost as if trying to keep the horror trapped inside her; oh God, her father had to mention a rat! Those things skitter around with their wet little raw noses sniffing around, their tiny little horrible toenails etching a reminder into the floors; oh Lord Jesus, that was what was happening inside her! Only it was a squirrel, just like any other probably—

"The only embarrassment this family ever did suffer was a slacker of a man like yourself! If you wasn't such a shiftless, no account—"

"Oh, it's me now, is it?"

"You're damn straight! You're damn straight!"

"Oh it's me now is it?!"

"You're damn straight it is, you no account bum! Making the children go out and work to pick up your slack? Uh-uh, it ain't right!"

"*I'll* be the one to decide what's right around here Ernestine."

...oh God, the squirrels, they have those sharp teeth that carve nuts open—her insides were being carved open! No wonder she was in so much pain! Ever since that one morning last month, that was when the pain had begun. The night before she had left the window open, just like she normally did when the house got too stuffy. There were times when she liked to watch the squirrels creeping around on the window sill, but none had ever come into the house before.

Quadira's mother was so beside herself with disgust that she picked up a plate and threw it to the floor with great violence, only with the carpeting it wasn't quite enough force, so in her frenzy she snatched it up again. Her second tantrum proved more successful and the plate shattered, with one of the slivers even darting across to where Quadira sat, embedding itself in her leg, but in her state of mind she failed to noticed it. Josephine, seven years Quadira's junior at the age of five, began to cry over in the corner where she huddled.

With hands on hips Quadira's father snidely laughed. "I sure ain't the one's got to clean that mess up woman. Hell, why not, let's all bust up the house!" So saying he cast his mug into a suicide trajectory, allowing the thing to burst against the corner cupboard.

That was the only reasonable explanation to it all as far as Quadira could tell, the window theory. One of those furry little things had snuck in while she was sleeping, rummaged about in her room maybe, then crept into her bed looking for a place to hide. Maybe it was a rat?! No, no, Quadira could not allow herself to believe such a thing. It must have been a squirrel, and somehow that gross little thing had gotten inside of her, got trapped, and was trying to chew its way to freedom. If there was an Almighty He would spare her any more pain, prevent any more bloodshed, put a solution to this horror in her mind so that she might eliminate it once and for all.

"You gone asked for it now July! I don't care no more, I just do not care!" Quadira's mother stooped then to pick up the thorn brach that lay beside Malcolm.

"Don't you do it woman. You hear me Ernestine?"

Her mother cried out just then, having pricked herself on one of the thorns. Malcom's body convulsed at that moment, rising vertically at least a foot, before bouncing on the floor and shooting up to a standing position with a howl. Both parents were sent reeling by this action; Malcom's screams, combined with the rivulets of bloody urine-mud he had flung about during his ghastly resurrection, proved enough to silence the household. Just as quickly he went silent again, simply standing still, staring straight ahead at the finger-painting Josephine had taped to the wall.

Even Quadira had been roused from her internal torments momentarily. She soon lost interest, however. Maybe when Malcolm was inside her chewing her guts out she could spare him the time of day. Until then she had to devise some plan for exterminating the invading rodent.

Quadira's mother was the first to find her voice. "Praise be..."

$ $ $

Josephine was confused, as always. When did her parents not confuse her? After listening to her father's rants about being "the have-nots" day in and day out, at the dinner table, in the bathroom, on the rooftop, she had taken him literally. In school, on the first day when everybody was watching her, and the teacher asked, "Little girl, what's your name please? You didn't respond to the roll call..." Josephine had proudly announced that her last name was Havenot. To this day she still didn't understand why the other kids had all laughed, or why her teachers refused to call her Josephine Havenot. Now her brother was risen from the drainage ditch, risen from Death's grasp. Or was he? "Malc alive?" she timidly asked her mother.

"Oh! What kind of question is that?!" her mother screamed, tearing at her own hair, engulfed by ravenous happiness.

"I'll be damned, I'll be damned, I'll be damned!" Josephine's father shouted, standing, hurling his rolled up paper at the floor with deadly intent. "What now? What now?! We ain't been put upon enough? We ain't got bills to pay and taxes to pay and worries enough for our boy to up and die, then come back up in here like some kinda undead freak?!"

"Don't you talk that way!" Josephine's mother hollered, her sheltering arms thrown around Malcolm despite all the icky stuff on him.

"I'll talk that way! I'll talk that way and more! You wanna go and die boy? Well? Well! Then you keep on goin'! I didn't give your butt permission, did I, to come on back in my house, see? We don't *have* no undead in here! Uh-uh!"

Was her brother alive or dead? What did "undead" mean exactly?

Josephine's mother did something then, something she had not witnessed before: she snarled, lips drawn back in a feral grimace while a strangled sound emanated from her throat.

"Don't give me that, woman. Look at us! Just when we had one less mouth to feed, and now what? My God, we are the have-nots, I'll tell you, those mansion-livin' sons of bitches don't have to put up with this nonsense. I'm the have-notingest bastard on this lump of mud spinnin' through space towards Armageddon, that's what I am!"

So did that mean her older brother Malcolm was some kind of angel now, or maybe a devil who slipped into bodies like they were pajamas? He didn't look evil, or overly good either, he just sort of looked like, well, Malcolm. She wandered over to the center of the room where he was located and stood waving her hand back and forth through his line of vision. There was no visible indication that anything registered.

"Don't you do that honey child, you go on and leave your brother alone now. And you, July, you need to shut that mouth before the flies get out. Who ever said our Malcolm was dead? Well? You a doctor now *and* a layabout?"

Just then Josephine's oldest sister, DeAnne, who hadn't been home for days—probably because she dropped out of tenth grade earlier in the week—came barging in through the front door, listening to music through headphones and singing along. "What it is what it is, this freaky bitch *is*, back in da hizzouse like Mickey-Mickey-Mizzouse, step to my grill an' I'll rip yo skanky blizzouse, I take your man home and make 'im, make 'im shizzout, those funky high-waters you got is—"

"*Dee!*" both of Josephine's parents yelled, their eyes and veins nearly bursting. At that moment the entire family froze, the only sound audible being that of the music blasting out of DeAnne's headphones. After a long, uncomfortable pause Josephine's father finally turned back on her mother like a dog driven mad. "Woman, you want to keep that brokedown walkin' corpse then you get his stank self cleaned, and then you put yourself to work down here cleanin' up the mess—"

"July—"

"Shut your mouth Ernestine—"

"July—"

While Josephine's parents reached a feverish level of malice DeAnne stood speechless and Quadira just kept rocking back and forth like she had all evening. Josephine used a twig to poke at Malcolm, poke him in the chest and the throat and then the face, but he never flinched, never even looked at her.

"Oh stop that!" her mother yelled, knocking the twig from her grasp.

Quadira leapt up, oblivious to the scene, and raced to the kitchen which was still in disarray from the practice session with the thorn switch. She threw open the cabinets under the sink, where all the cleaning chemicals were stored, and began to wildly fling containers left and right, discarding them on the vinyl tiling.

"What in creation is going on now?" Josephine's father exclaimed. "What it going on in that child's head? Ernestine, get your daughter under control!"

Finally Quadira stood, almost throwing herself down in her haste, her hands clamped around a cylindrical pesticide container with a pump handle. "*Kill the squirrel!*" she screamed, plunging the contraption between her legs.

On seeing this everyone sprang into motion simultaneously, all save for Malcolm that is. Josephine made it to her sister first, struggling in vain to turn her around in an effort to see what was going on.

The rest of the family, however, had plans of a different nature, and arrived only a split second after the diminutive girl. Their parents wrestled the cylinder away from the raving twelve-year-old, threw her back, pinned her to the table.

With the music still pumping from under her earphones DeAnne jumped forward, landing a blow to Quadira's face, followed by another and another, and everybody in the family was too shocked by the many turns of events to make any attempt to curtail the beating. "You sick little skeeza, I ain't even *tryin'* to see that, I ain't even tryin' to see that!" she kept repeating as she pounded Quadira.

Finally Josephine's father intervened, his fingers brutally crushing DeAnne's exposed shoulders, decimating the skin, and he slapped her like God smacking a stray rebel angel back down to the fiery depths...*and he had that look in his eye.* "What is wrong with this family?" he uttered, not really seeing them anymore. "You're all against me, aren't you? Yeah...yeah..they are...got to stand up for myself..."

"Don't! Don't you go doing nothing rash now, honey," Josephine's mother said, attempting to come off as soothing, while DeAnne collected herself on the floor. Quadira wailed unintelligibly on the table; Malcolm was petrified in the living room; Josephine was confused again. *What squirrel?* "July honey, don't you do nothing rash now, you know we all love Daddy...ain't that right girls? Tell your papa."

Josephine's father was far from listening though. He shambled out of the room, world-worn, in search of something. It seemed as though he may have been grunting something under his breath, but he might not have been.

Did Josephine have two dead brothers now? Was that the truth or did she just make it up? Nobody ever mentioned her oldest brother, her parents wouldn't tolerate such talk. All that she knew about him was that he was the second oldest, right after DeAnne. Maybe he was just visiting somewhere for a long time, or at one of those fancy schools where you sleep and eat there year-round. All Josephine knew was that she wanted to know more but probably never would.

$ $ $

Hershel was in several thousand pieces by this point, on a shelf overlooking the dining room, his ashes in an oversized plastic martini cup, covered with plastic wrap that had grown loose with time. Hershel's present situation was on account of his father having sold the brass urn he came home in for what turned out to be a decent profit.

$ $ $

When the old man had thrown DeAnne down he had been lucky, because she wasn't expecting him to act up. Otherwise she would've let him know that things had changed. She collected herself up off the floor, the music still pounding an outrage in her ears. Her mother was motionless, not even paying any attention to her, just standing there staring after the old man like she'd been doing her whole adult life. That freak Quadira was preoccupied with sobbing on the kitchen table, still as helpless as DeAnne had left her. Josephine just kept saying "What's goin' on?" over and over again and that little Erkle wannabe Malcolm kept his vigil in the living room.

Whatever was going on in the home didn't matter; DeAnne would set things square with the pops and then either split or take things over. Feeling up the lead she was packing, DeAnne had more than half a mind to just blow up the spot once and for all. She had her clique in full effect so what was the point of even trying to stay there anyway?

"July!" her mother called, nervously.

"Just let him try something," DeAnne reassured herself.

DeAnne's mother grabbed at her arm. "Don't tell me that man hit you hard enough to knock the sense out of your head. Don't you go provoking nothing now, girl."

"What's wrong with Quadira mama?" Josephine asked.

"This family," was DeAnne's answer.

The old man's footsteps vibrated through the staircase and interrupted her mother's scolding words. By the time he made it down the stairs DeAnne was prepared, much to her mother's horror. At first she thought her father was rolling with a gauge but no, it was just a rifle. He must have sold the shotgun sometime and picked this thing up to replace it. Either that or he'd done something that required him to dispose of it discreetly. At that moment, though, he was bug-eyed, the rifle still slung over his shoulder, not at all prepared for what his daughter had in store.

"That's right pops, you starin' at the trey-eight. What'chu gotta say now big man?"

Well, he certainly hadn't expected to have a .38 caliber handgun leveled at him. "You going to play it like that? Huh girl?"

"Best believe it."

"Dee honey," her mother said, cringing. "Why don't you—"

"Shut up Ernestine! I knew you was against me, alla yous, so drop the damn act! Pointing a gun at a man in his own home..."

DeAnne wanted to pull the trigger right then. "You ain't the only one livin' here old man!" The two of them stood motionless, staring at each other with deadly intent. Mad doggin' it in the streets was one thing but to do it in your own home, well, it was kind of surreal. That behavior had to start somewhere though. Her brothers and sisters weren't any baby G's, but they were hard enough to take care of themselves if the caps started going off like the Fourth of July. They would have to be, or else they'd get blasted. It was that simple, just like in the streets. Get smart quick or get dead quicker.

Without warning Quadira unleashed a blood-churning scream at which their father jumped, aiming his gun in the general direction of the kitchen. DeAnne wasted no time firing, but with Malcolm standing where he was she had to let it fly way too high. Everyone began screaming simultaneously in the moments that followed, running and diving for cover. The shot served its purpose: the old fool stumbled back toward the front door, bungling his effort to load the rifle in the process. Only Malcolm remained untouched by the shocking noise.

"Where you goin'? Where you goin'?" DeAnne yelled while charging at the front windows. "Come on back in here, I got some more for you!" No sooner had she finished the sentence than a bullet came rocketing through the front wall. Suddenly the lights went out—somebody had the presence of mind to at least do that much—and all hell broke loose under the cover of darkness. There were assorted cries accompanied by the sounds of objects being bumped into or knocked over. Some fool tried to wrench the gun out of DeAnne's grip, a move which prompted her to go ahead and take up a position upstairs like she had been contemplating. If she stayed down there with that lot they'd end up making her shoot one of them by accident.

She shoved the framed photos off the dresser by the window in her parents' room. While standing by the bunched up drapes she became distracted by thoughts of grammar lessons and all the stupid books they made you read in school. Who gave a damn about a bunch of fake people or dead people, and just what the hell was "tripping the light fantastic" supposed to mean anyway?

"Damn!" the old fool hollered outside. "Damn it, God *damn* it!"

Damn, *slam*, ka-blam Viet*nam*, that's Uncle Sam, ya know how he ran, get off the bandwagon and join the caravan, grab a baseball bat and *splat*...no way, she had to stop thinking about the rhymes and get serious about this shoot-out with her father. For some reason those same lyrics kept coming back to her over and over while she nervously peered out from behind the blinds. No, it wasn't that she was nervous about the old man, no way. At last she finally turned off the CD player and threw the headphones to the side.

"You hearin' me in there?! Huh?! I'm a'burn this place down!"

In response DeAnne fired a shot into the cluster of trash cans her father was hiding behind, succeeding only in sending old food flying all over. No way had any of them thought it would come to this. Thinking about the steps she had taken over the years to get into her current series of screw-ups only made her head hurt. All she she knew was that the hardcore lifestyle spiraled like this until she finally found herself busting caps at her own father in the middle of the house with the family still inside. Who knew whether her little brother or sisters would be around to see the sunrise? Maybe it was a bit late for her to be realizing all this. Then again maybe not...

She yelled out hoping her father would respond. "We can end it with caps or end it with words..." DeAnne never thought of herself as a negotiator. Normally she would just fly off the handle no matter how many reasonable alternatives were available.

Somewhere a dog was barking aimlessly, a car alarm began to sound, a baby began to cry. One or two porch lights flickered on but no one dared step outside. Muffled sobs made their way up to DeAnne from downstairs. From the trash cans, nothing.

At the end of her patience she demanded, "So what it be?!"

$ $ $

Ernestine was glad to be past all the chaos and anger and police reports. She tried to relax, to fade into the chair, into the moment. This was her favorite time, the calm hours that fell between the weekend's trifles. There would usually be a pretty good lull between about two-thirty and five o'clock each day when everyone just slept or read the paper or was out doing whatever it was they did with their friends. She simply sat contentedly in her favorite chair, a real plush number they had rescued from somebody's trash a couple years back, in the wee hours before the trash men could claim it. During the last six days she had nearly grown into the chair, forming a symbiotic relationship with the thing. As much work as knitting was, Ernestine would be spending a considerable amount of time there in the next eight or so months.

The news people were covering some kind of well-to-do event in Europe. A beat-up guy in a tuxedo and a bad wig was before a gathering of reporters, smiling, his beautiful wife and daughter standing beside him sullenly. July attacked the television then, dislodging it from its resting place, shouting, "That Pretorious sumbitch! That Pretorious sumbitch! Let him come down here from his cushy-ass life and pretty family, let him try livin' up in this hole for a while! I don't wanna see these damn rich-folk! No rich-folk! No more rich-folk! Don't show it to me no more! I don't wanna see their fancy, happy lives...it's crap! You hear me? Crap!"

The television was unable to reply, beaten senseless as it was, sitting at an odd angle with rolling static its only offering. Ernestine was only capable of shaking her head and giving the caustic admonition, "Well, now, you ought to be proud of yourself July. I do believe that TV learned its lesson." Suddenly, alarmingly sobered, he stood and stared at her for a bit, not replying. Instead, he opted to return to his chair and shut his mouth like he should've done long ago. In the meantime Ernestine wondered why he didn't comment on what were obviously shaping up to be baby clothes. "I'll tell you why!" she said boldly, jolting the man just as he had settled in. But he refused to inquire, instead picking up his newspaper and pulling the edges tight several times so that it made that disgusting flapping noise she so despised.

Yes, this would be a snug little outfit for her first grandchild. It was true, she was concerned that Quadira was starting a bit too young; after all Ernestine herself had at least been fifteen when she gave birth to DeAnne. Could it be that she should have given her little girl the birds and the bees talk, and the talk about the transition to womanhood? No, she was so young! Ernestine kept thinking that something should have been done differently but couldn't figure out what. Maybe this "squirrel," as her daughter called it, would do the family some good, give them something positive to focus on for once. Squirrel. Hmm, yep, she thought, that may make a good name, come boy or girl child. In fact maybe that's what Quadira had in mind all along! Why, yes, that must have been it.

Thankfully all that nastiness from earlier in the week had settled down. Little Dee-Dee and July both had stayed at neutral homes while things cooled off; the police grudgingly accepted her explanation of an accident while cleaning the family gun. Although her husband and eldest child had yet to reach rapprochement there was more than enough room in the household for them to stew independent of each other's presence. More than that, it seemed as though cooler heads might prevail because just that morning July had fixed himself a glass of orange juice while Dee ate her cereal in the same room. "Praise be!"

July grudgingly looked her way, grimacing once or twice, then got up and set to fixing the television. "Damn Japanese clap-trappin' contraption!"

"I don't think the Japs came and knocked that thing cock-eyed, July."

"You stick to what you know best woman, and I'll stick to what I know."

"Looks like the only thing you know is how to go busting up this house. And another thing—"

"I done told you to stick to what you know woman, which is just to sit there and shut your mouth."

"Why, of all the—"

Just then Dee entered the room and for one tense moment Ernestine honestly thought there would be bloodshed. Instead her daughter pretended not to see anything out of place. "I'm going out," she told them.

"Well go on then," July grunted.

On the way to the door Dee stopped. "What's up with this?" she said, nudging the length of thorn bush.

"The new family enterprise. See, Malcolm and me are turning into enterprisers here. People always got somebody what needs a good whipping. So, we go around arranging such and Malcolm whips 'em. Ten bucks per job."

"Whippin' on peoples? I'll do it better than that little boy ever could." Already she was putting on the work gloves.

"No, no, that there's men's work," July cautioned. "Why don't you just sit still for once and try to be lady-like. Help your mother out with that baby-knitting stuff."

"Why can't you be civil for once!" Ernestine shrieked. This outburst did not command the attention she had hoped for, and the two went about ignoring the family matriarch.

"Malcolm, get yourself down here," July called.

"Split it half and half," Dee said. "I know plenty of people needing to get a reality check."

Ernestine continued griping, but July only yelled louder for Malcolm to get his butt down there. Dee was talking some mumbo jumbo about being able to make two hundred bucks a day off this business and it altogether gave Ernestine a disheartening feeling. How could a mother fall out of the emotional radar of her family? Dropped like a fly, she had. A mother should be the center of a family, the rock, the foundation she told herself. Eventually theiu unsettlingly silent son meandered downstairs and July grabbed his whipping equipment.

"I'm a regular Jackie O," Ernestine grumbled to nobody.

"What now?" July demanded to know, sounding as though he had been harassed to the ends of the world by mangy dogs.

"Oh nothin'. You just keep on doin'."

"I swear woman. Sometimes...I swear." He could only shake his head and drag Malcolm out into the yard.

$ $ $

From the warmth of her bed Quadira could hear her father grouching at her little brother and knew that after a week off they were back at it again. She did not want to be hearing their masculine foolishness, their violent words and actions that summoned only disquieting feelings. The last few days had gone by without a thought anchoring itself in her head, which is to say they were good days. She had spent the better part of the week locked away in the confines of that pink room, hiding from reality under the darkness provided by blanket after blanket. Still though, some troubling things lingered.

Quadira's mother had told her she would be giving birth sometime down the road, all too soon, as incomprehensible as it was to her mind. Quadira could only focus on finding some way to escape the sick fate awaiting her, but no one ventured any helpful thoughts on the matter. The horror was too great to face and just thinking of it made Quadira bury her head in the pillows and blankets all over again. No, she told herself. She couldn't let the squirrel win. She had to get herself out of that bed and do something to help herself. Her first sight after throwing back the covers was that of her window. It was propped wide open and sitting right on the window sill, on its hind quarters, was a squirrel gnawing away at a nut.

On seeing a squirrel perched there she unleashed a scream from the depths of her soul. She leapt from the bed, nearly ripping her nightshirt on the rusty edges of the old trunk next to the window. Without hesitation she slammed the window shut, the space empty because the squirrel had fled at her first sound. Over and over Quadira screamed, unable to control herself, unable to calm down.

She wondered what would the birth be like. No, her mama had never given her "the talk" that some other girls referred to, or told her what being a mother entailed, but there was no mistake about what was happening to her. Sitting there on the messed up old trunk she tried not to think of anything, anything at all, as anything that came to her mind could break it in two at that moment.

"Honey-child?" her mother called from down the hallway. "Quadira?" she called, drawing closer. "Baby, mother wants to talk to you," she said, too close.

Quadira did her best to normalize herself before her mother entered the room. "Yes Mama." She met her mother at the door; the woman was beside herself with happiness.

"You okay up here girl? Sounded like I heard something a minute ago..."

"No, no mama, I'm okay," Quadira was quick to say, followed by, "The beast didn't get me," in a barely audible voice.

"That's good dear. Now you listen. I have something for you. Something what's gonna cheer you right up."

"You...you got something for me?"

"That's right. A present." Her mother held the cute, fuzzy little outfit up with pride. It was yellow with the word "SQUIRREL" across the front in huge red letters. Quadira stepped away, gasping on seeing this. Even her mother sided with the vermin that invaded her body, tore at her guts! Her mother chuckled, obviously happy with her work and the thought of a grandchild. "Oh, you don't need to say nothing darling. We'll just put this away for safe keeping until we have our little 'Squirrel' here with us."

"Squirrels...squirrels are okay?"

"Honey, that little bright-eyed and bushy-tailed baby will be loved in this house, and don't pay no never mind to whatever your daddy might be saying. And I think Squirrel is an adorable name, boy or girl."

Quadira was stupefied by this turn of events. "You do?" She had at least thought her mother would assist her in her time of unspeakable need. "Oh, Mama, don't—"

"Shh, shh, it's okay darling," her mother was telling her. The woman wrapped her arms around Quadira, murmuring all the while that things would be all right. Where Quadira was, though, she could no longer hear her mother's voice...only the chittering of rodents.

$ $ $

After word of Malcolm destroying Lowdown's dong spread through the surrounding area July's whipping scheme became the stuff of legend. Far as he could tell they had done a public service by banishing that stumblebum fool, and the way in which they had done it afforded them a certain window of opportunity. If he could launch his "whip your kid" campaign that weekend the profits would be enormous.

Things could be going better though. Malcolm seemed almost totally unresponsive to verbal commands lately. "What's wrong with you son? Got shit in your ears? I said swing that thing like you mean it!"

"July, you leave that boy alone," Ernestine called from the doorway. "Malcolm, you come here and stay home with your mother."

"This boy been on tit long enough, woman. Leave him to me. I'll make a man outta the boy yet." Dee lingered nearby looking skeptical, as usual. That sat well with July so long as she kept her nose out of his business. He had already instructed the boy on the fine art of presenting himself to a prospective sucker...the cutesy thing, that childish appeal stuff to make them shell out their money to some kid they didn't even know. That worked every time. "Right now, remember you gotta look like you're Denzel Washington out here." For whatever reason his son just didn't look convincing in the intimidation department. Who would buy this product? "Naw, boy, no way. Look at you. Listen, you wanna earn your keep, you better get this straight."

July had drilled his son for the better part of the afternoon already, and it only took a little while longer until he finally felt confident that they were presentable and coordinated as a team. When they left he noticed Quadira rocking back and fourth with her legs and arms crossed, up on one of the sturdier boughs of the nearest tree. Her smile gave him a shiver and her eyes—those dead, unfocused eyes—were directed at a crudely made trap of some sort only a few branches away. July thought better of trying to communicate with her at that point, instead keeping his mind on the task at hand.

Their first stop was at the Colby home. July had managed to forget the Colbys were out of town for the week so they had to keep on moving. And damn if DeAnne didn't keep sticking to them like white on black! "Girl, I already told you—"

"Yeah, yeah, men's work. Well why don't you just show me how it gets done then."

"Fine by me."

"Fine."

After that exchange they moved on to another black residence. This was one of the less popular places to be seen in the area, in fact many who drove past considered it an eyesore. The dilapidated structure housed who-knows-how-many people, but the one person July knew he did not want to see there was that wicked old wrinkly wreck of a human, allegedly a woman. The old woman idled on the porch seat flapping a sagging arm in the hopes of deterring the numerous flies.

July sidled up to the baggy old bat. “Hi.”

“What for?”

“Just speakin’.”

“Mm-hmm.” She sucked on her gums a bit and went back to ignoring him.

A series of creaks preceded a man pushing open the rusting screen door. July was relieved to have Porkchop on hand; another minute with that crazy old broad and he’d be a wanted man. Porkchop had certainly seen better days, and some worse, July imagined. He was wearing decades-old overalls with some sorry red longjohns underneath. The unsymetric clumps of hair on Porkchop’s head seemed to writhe.

“Hey there neighbor,” July offered. “Been a while.”

“What it be,” Porkchop said while flecks of beef and saliva jettisoned between his gray stumps of teeth. July noticed that the words GOOD LUVIN were etched on the breast of Porkchop’s overalls in blue ink. Porkchop seemed to notice something unusual. “What wrong with dat dere boy?”

“Whaddaya mean? My son here’s been blessed with insane health all his whole life long.”

Porkchop grumbled. “Sho’ ‘nuff.”

“Now whaddaya mean by that? What do you mean Porkchop?”

“Hey now! What’chu say my man?!” Nobody ever called him Porkchop to his face. His real name was something like Jeremiah.

“Listen here, I came to you today ‘cause of this here scam I’m runnin’, see?” If anything would get Porkchop’s attention back on track that was it.

"Come again?"

"That's right. The whippin' business. Go on, show 'em what I mean."

They all stood back and watched Malcolm while he remained still. He didn't pick up the thorns, he didn't even seem to register that July had indeed spoken to him. Worthless silence and an Earthy smell pervaded the scene, accompanied by distant sirens and a radio. Without warning Malcolm erupted. "*Crumbs!*" he shouted, fingers squirming, his features momentarily distorted before reverting back to his docile mode.

Stoically observing his son at arms' length July grunted and turned to the others. "The boy ain't right!"

"Sho' 'nuff. I already done say dat Jim."

It drove July mad that this bumpkin always had to refer to him as "Jim". "See, I rent the boy out to whip on people with that there thorn switch. You must'a heard what my son did to Lowdown." Both the toothless witch and Porkchop "Mm-hmm"ed in unison. "I need to generate some *steady* cash flow, dig? I'm talkin' 'bout white folk here. Now how does that strike you?"

"Shucks," Porkchop grunted, sliding his tongue in and out through the large gap between his teeth. Dee almost broke out right then and there but July gave her a silencing glare. "I dunno."

"Tell you what brother. You scope out any marks and I'll cut you in on the side, now what you say?"

"Hell if'n I be knowin' Jim. Dey all been lookin' da same to my ass, like dey done been drained a'dere blood an' shit like dat." Then, for emphasis, "Fuh."

Well, he was a stupid bamma to be sure, as far as July figured it, but he was one of the few black folk in the neighborhood.

"Shee. I you man, pardner." Porkchop grinned, the way animals at the zoo yawn their fangs into view. He wiped his hand on his blue jean posterior and offered it to July.

"Good lookin' out brother," July said, taking the foul man's sweaty hand and shaking it as little as possible. He eyed the old woman in the process, having not a smidgen of trust for her—it was rumored she had long been a practitioner of the black arts collectively known as voodoo. "Well now you come my way and let me know when you got somethin' for me."

Porkchop cackled and gestured behind him. "Ain't no need fuh dat. I got'cho mark right here..."

* * *

With everyone else out doing adult stuff Josephine was pretty much bored. She decided to check out the side of the house and see what Quadira was up to in the tree. Her older sister was still situated in the same place as before, facing away from her, just moving back and forth and occasionally shattering the silence with a coarse burst of giggles. "What'cha doin'?" Josephine had to ask this a few times before Quadira finally noticed her.

Without turning to face her Quadira replied, "Waiting for the beast..."

"The beast? What beast?" Already things were getting confusing.

Instead of answering, Quadira climbed down, carefully, her eyes darting all around as she descended. She drew in close to Josephine and hesitated before speaking. "There's somethin' horrible can happen to a girl," she gravely intoned. With quivering lips she struggled to continue. "A girl...can get infected by...by a squirrel, if she ain't been careful. Squirrels is evil sis, you always 'member that. They get inside and, and, and they claw at you and bite inside your tummy—" At that point Josephine insisted that Quadira stop because she was getting scared by all that talk. After a series of failed attempts to get her older sister to play dolls with her Quadira suddenly perked up. “Come on, let’s play house,” she suggested.

This couldn’t have made Josephine happier. Malcolm was useless for playing and DeAnne was just so above her sisters. “I get to bake the cake,” Josephine declared as she let Quadira guide her behind the trash heap in the back yard. Finally they stopped at the very edge of their property.

“You’ll be safe from them squirrels in here sis...” Quadira held the door open for her then and Josephine just knew that her sister had nothing but the best in mind for her.

“Is that the Havenot house?” Josephine asked, feeling better, wanting to play with her sister.

“Yeah. This here is the Havenot house. You Josephine Havenot?”

“Yes’m.”

“Well I expect you better get on in your house then.” Quadira paused for a moment, adding, “Before the squirrels get you!”

“I told you to stop sayin’ that!”

“Then get yourself inside and hush up.”

“What about you?”

“I’ll be along soon enough...sooner than I want...but you go on ahead in there. Go on, I’ll be joinin’ you soon enough.”

Josephine eyed the inside, feeling strange about it for some reason. “I don’t know Quadira. I don’t know...”

Quadira put her hands on her hips in a valiant effort to impersonate their mother. “Don’t you want to see Herschel, girl?”

“Is that...is he my brother?”

“That’s right. Don’t you want to see your brother?”

“Yeah! Where is he?! You know where he at?” Josephine could not believe her fortune, that she could finally meet the mysterious brother whom she had never known.

"Don't you worry your head about that right now. Just get on in here and wait for me to come back for you." Josephine meekly complied and stepped inside. Quadira did something odd then; before closing the door she kissed Josephine on the forehead. "Bye, little sis."

"I'll see you in a little while," Josephine replied. Then it was dark, very dark, and the door was closed all the way.

Their parents had told them a million billion times not to play in or around the ancient refrigerator because, well, she wasn't sure why but...just because Mom had said so. Josephine trusted her big sister though, even if she had been acting a little strange lately. So she would wait, in her own special Havenot House, sort of like that charity thing the fast food chain always advertised during cartoon time on Saturdays, yeah, except it was all for her.

$ $ $

Hershel remained on the shelf where they had left him, immobile. Everyone was out, doing who-knows-what, when the sound of a window being forced open invaded the silence. A person, a stranger, crept in with a string of quiet obscenities on his lips.

"Kill 'em muthafuck," the man mumbled to no one. Several grunts and rumbles followed as he shambled around the house, unable to locate any of the family members. He was dressed in filthy clothes which had been worn thin and heavily stained by blood, among other things. The knife he held with reverence was long, sharp, double-edged with a thick black handle, most likely a hunting knife. "Where is 'ey?" The man followed this comment with a howl of pain when he inadvertently took too large a step. After gripping his crotch for several minutes he moved on, finding the liquor cabinet. The little sounds of animalistic glee trapped between his teeth were tempered with intermittent grunts of pain as he alternately grabbed bottles and his groin.

"Wait for 'em," he said, happily plopping himself down at the dinner table and stabbing his blade into the chair next to him. The stranger seemed to try and drink himself to ruin then, taking healthy samples of each poison until his mutterings were nearly incomprehensible. After well over an hour a gust of wind thrashed the screen door and, thinking that the family was returning, the liquored-up stranger yanked his knife out of the chair—with some difficulty—and wielded it about with deadly inaccuracy. He nearly fell on his face several times while swinging the frightening blade back and forth in his limp grasp. Finally satisfied that nobody was there to be killed he drooped back into a recumbant position. "Stab 'em...chop on 'em cockses..."

At that moment he spied Hershel. "Oh, uht's 'is? Huh..." The struggle to rise to his feet did not best him and eventually he managed to cross over to the shelf. "Uh mix!" he said, his eyes wide with excitement. Without hesitation he grabbed the martini glass and returned to his treasure trove of alcohol. "Uh mix! Uh mix!" He whipped the plastic wrap off, spilling a portion of Hershel's ashes in his haste. Deciding that gin would be the best thing the man clumsily opened the bottle and poured a measure in, then a bit more, stirring his concoction with the knife blade. "'Em muthafuck got 'em uh mix...hee-hee! Not nuh mo'," he said and, not caring whether all the flakes and crumbs were fully dissolved, he downed Hershel and the gin in one protracted, slovenly exhibition of glugging.

$ $ $

"Go on now boy. And don't be shaming me."

Malcolm marched on up to the intimidating door exactly the way his father had told him to. Without even looking back at his father Malcolm banged on the door rhythmically, robotically. Within a few moments footsteps could be heard inside, approaching erratically.

The door opened to reveal a suburban housewife. The woman was long, pale, with dark hair and an incredibly angular face, and her overall image reminded Malcolm of a scythe. That is, if a scythe were kept in an ugly flower print dress. Up beyond the peak of her nose the dark eyes turned down to him. He stood there doing his best to give an appearance of gladiatorial innocence. "Hello there little boy. I think you must have the wrong house."

Malcolm's father intervened just then. "Good afternoon ma'am," he said from a distance, grinning. "We come to you today to offer a service."

"A service?"

"Yes," Malcolm's father replied. Stepping forward he continued, "A highly specialized service for your family."

"I'm not sure that we are especially in need of any services today, thank you." Those long, huge, fake curls of hers refused to move even slightly when she spoke.

"Oh now, I know what you're thinking ma'am, but I'll let you be assured that these are no ordinary services. We can today offer services for your family that most white folk may not be accustomed to, something that we are now willing to share, for the first time, at an affordable price."

A man's voice called from inside, "I say, what is this all about?"

The bleached or embalmed woman finally turned her gaunt frame away from them. "Oh, it's nothing dear."

"Really now? It does not sound like just 'nothing' to me." Soon enough the man was at the doorway. He was a bespectacled Caucasian fellow wearing suspenders and smoking one of those pipes that Sherlock Holmes made famous.

"Good afternoon mister..."

"McCreedy, Greg McCreedy's the name."

"Right, Mr. McCreedy. My name is July, and my son and I come to you today to offer a wonderful innovative service for a nominal fee. My son will perform ten lashes of the thorn whip on a person of your choosing for only ten dollars. They will be whipped on the face, yes, directly on the face."

"Whipped?!"

"Yes sir, on the face, directly on the face, and other extremities of the body *if you will.*"

"Oh, honey," Mrs. McCreedy giggled, attempting to cover her mouth. Obviously she didn't take this seriously for a single moment.

"If you wish, we can provide a quick demonstration..."

"All right there July, I'm a fair man. Let me view your wares."

Malcolm's father stood back. "Give it a go son, just like you did Lowdown."

For reasons beyond his grasp thoughts of his lessons on the French Revolution flooded Malcolm's mind until the images of old-time Europeans struggling and killing each other were all that he could see. "Yah!" he cried, exploding with violence as he lashed out with the switch. What he experienced were the screams of foreigners to whose paleness he added some color...red, a dark, thick red. "Come on redskins!" he shrieked. "Yah! Crumbs!"

"Well now, I'll say," Mr. McCreedy procclaimed, puffing appreciatively on his Sherlock pipe. "The boy certainly is vicious enough, I'll give him that." Chuckles followed all around. "I don't know what you people do to them to turn them into maddened beasts but I'll say, you've got my compliments. Okay, I'll bite. How much did you say your service costs?"

"It's a nominal fee of just thirteen dollars."

Mrs. McCreedy was shocked by the conversation taking place yet she kept silent. Her husband digested what Malcolm's father said and asked, "How many lashes does that get me? Ten, if I am not mistaken."

"Aw now Mr. McCreedy, being an upstanding member of the neighborhood as such, I think we can manage a few extra for you."

"Splendid! I'm sold. Honey, go fetch Chipper and Morley for me.

I'll take two." Mrs. McCreedy didn't move a muscle, just like the corpse Malcolm imagined her to be. "Go on honey, I've made up my mind." While Malcolm savaged a barren patch of yard with the thorns Mrs. McCreedy stomped inside to, presumably, retrieve the boys.

"Two orders Mr. McCreedy?" Malcolm's father asked, taking out a pencil and pad of paper to write it all down.

"Absolutely July. I'll tell you, both of my lads need some discipline. Maybe a few sessions with your boy here will get them every bit as vicious as him."

"Two orders," Malcolm's father chuckled while slowly writing. "Thank you kindly Mr. McCreedy. I hope you will understand that all our transactions have to be made in cash."

"I suppose you require payment upfront, eh?"

"Something like that."

"As a great man once said, 'this is not a problem'; I want to see this." The man counted out the appropriate money and handed it over just as Chipper and Morley were dragged from the house by their mother.

Malcolm had known of them since they moved into the neighborhood two years ago. They didn't attend the same school. No, the McCreedy boys were purely boarding school stock. Even so they had developed a bit of a reputation among the other children. Their habits were the stuff best discussed in whispers with no adults around. Morley started up with, "What's this all about? I was just about to save the princess Dad."

Mr. McCreedy removed the pipe from his mouth. "Confound those stupid video games—"

"Honey—" Mrs. McCreedy began.

"Not now Celia. Listen to me boys. You both know well enough what this is all about. Your contrivances will not get you out of this jam. Now take off your shirts and shut your mouths."

"Dad!"

"No back-talk! It's already been decided."

"Honey, they're just children!" Mrs. McCreedy interjected. Malcolm didn't care what happened so long as he got to perform.

"Yes, well, children need discipline. If not they grow up to be out of control."

"This is more than just *discipline*—"

McCreedy was tiring of the whole affair. "If you don't have the stomach for it don't watch!"

"Go on in boys, you don't have to do this!"

"No, you'll stand there and feast on your just deserts young men," McCreedy demanded.

"You give 'em their money's worth," Malcolm's father whispered to him.

Blinded by enticing visions of European agony Malcolm cut loose, whipping the McCreedy family dog simply because it happened to be there. While the thing yipped and hopped around in the dust both Mr. and Mrs. McCreedy sprang to life with an assortment of cries and admonitions.

"By jove, stop it I say!" Mr. McCreedy shouted while gesturing with his pipe. "The boy is quite obviously mad! We'll have no more of this!"

"Stop him!" the morose corpse of a woman hollered.

"As a civilized man I demand that you stop this at once! Further more I demand my money ba—" and, before he could finish, Malcolm unleashed the whip on Mrs. McCreedy herself, snagging the gaudy flower print shroud and ripping it to shreds. All hell broke loose the moment her black lingerie and chalk flesh were exposed to the light of day.

Malcolm's father, shuddering at having to see a white woman, dived for Malcolm but just wasn't fast enough to catch the ghost-whip-per. McCreedy went into such a frenzy, trying to subdue anything which happened to move, that he popped his suspenders. Malcolm couldn't see what his own family members were doing but the McCreedy woman passed out, the spirit keeping her lifeless body upright having fled after his righteous onslaught. Morley stood frozen, staring at his mother with a slack jaw, finally saying, "*Whoa mama!*" before being whipped on the face by his young black counterpart. At least Malcom had finally managed to do something right, something for which his father would lavish pride on him.

$ $ $

Well damn, DeAnne thought to herself. Now ain't that some shit! She knew that she should have packed the lead just in case shit got hectic and, just as she had suspected, it had gotten hectic with a quickness. It was only the first job even! But what had she told them? She'd seen her father screw up things with his hair-brained schemes in the past and this was no exception.

In the heat of the moment, frustrated at not being able to catch the outlandish terrier mix, Mr. McCreedy turned on DeAnne, grabbing her by the shoulders and heaving her back against the aluminum siding. Without hesitation DeAnne headbutted the man, smashing his face, driving him to thrash her about with escalating violence. The back of her head smacked against the wall repeatedly and the white man's hands were not in appropriate places, a fact which earned him a knee to the nuts.

"*Oh no you don't!*" her father shouted while tackling the McCreedy man. His momentum carried both men through the lovely bay windows and into the living room where albino hamsters ran in circles, trapped inside a gimmicky habitat shaped like a coffin.

That wannabe narc and her father could go kill each other for all DeAnne cared. She rushed forward to set things straight with

Malcolm. He was unleashing lash after lash, holding the white boys at bay while their mother chased the dog around the yard screaming her head off. “Come on,” DeAnne told her little brother.

Malcolm just shrugged her off and swung his weapon at Morley, catching the crying boy on the leg. The thorns became entangled in the fabric of his blue jeans. Chipper took his first action during the fray and yanked Morley free of the thorns, perhaps doing more damage to his brother than good.

“Barkley! Barkley! My God, come back here Barkley!” Mrs. McCreedy screamed while she and the dog wore a circle into the ground.

“Yah! Yah!”

“Come on Malcolm, you dumbass!”

Inside the house the men made it to their feet. The McCreedy man had managed to get a slew of teeth knocked out by being stupid enough to fight with a pipe clenched in his mouth. DeAnne’s father looked the better of the two, although both had multiple lacerations from going through the bay windows. They each teetered, high on adrenaline and pain, their limbs shaking and their wills infirm as they stood at the junction of attack or retreat.

In the meantime Chipper had gotten his hands on some stray rocks and began to cast them in Malcolm's direction. The little demon of a brother swung his whip with all his might but Chipper skipped about, just out of reach. During the pelting of stones Malcolm remained seemingly impervious to pain, not flinching once under the assault.

As if all that had transpired were not more than enough DeAnne found the dog had decided to tear at her leg with its wet jaws. In its pain the creature jumped every which way it could, all four paws leaving the ground, each tug sending a sharp sensation through her.

If only she had packed the trey-eight, she cried inwardly. Her first few attempts to kick the thing away from her were unsuccessful but Malcolm whipped it again, sending it running. The McCreedy woman came running at him full speed, ready to attack with claws and teeth, but DeAnne rocked her head with a left hook.

Without waiting to see if her attack felled the woman DeAnne grabbed both Malcolm and her stumbling father, dragging them toward the edge of the property. If one of those white folk wasn't already calling the Man down on them surely people in the bordering homes had put in a 911. Soon enough the man and boy stopped resisting her efforts to extricate them and the shouts and threats and wails began to fade into the distance.

$ $ $

Ernestine was returning from the week's grocery shopping with about thirteen bags full of hutchcome. No, it did not seem like anybody was home, not until she noticed Quadira in the tree. As usual the taxi driver did not help her unload the bags, and Quadira did not notice her mother's plight. That was typical for the family, not helping the mother and just sitting by idly while she struggled and struggled and nearly broke her back.

Quadira was preoccupied with torturing the one squirrel that had fallen for her trap. She slid a sharpened twig in and out of the cage and animal simultaneously while the little demon squealed. "How's it feel, squirrel?" she asked it contentedly, still rocking back and forth, without the manic vigor she had earlier. "*How's it feel now?*"

"What on Earth are you doing?!" Ernestine shrieked. Her daughter did not respond. "Quadira? You hear me?" The driver was shaking his head, a bit dismayed. "What're you lookin' at?" The man began to laugh instead of saying anything of substance. "Hey you! That there taxi ain't so nice as all that. I want my tip back. You give me that money back!" Ernestine was too slow to catch him though. The taxi screeched out of the driveway in reverse, over a bag full of dairy products, and continued half a block before shifting into drive and speeding into the distance. "Son of a bitch!" she yelled in frustration.

At the periphery of her vision were movements, the fast motions of people on the run: the rest of her family. They were a dejected lot returning home with their tails between their legs from the looks of it. As they drew closer she could make out numerous injuries, causing alarm to blind her to all else. Her concerned questions were rebuffed by the sullen threesome who hardly even acknowledged her, so she figured they must be okay after all. The only thing that seemed to move them was the bag of crushed groceries.

"Damn," July muttered. "Now how you like them apples?" Ernestine recounted the tale of the brigand at the controls in the taxi, much to the disgust of her family. "Son of a bitch. As if we don't have enough put upon us." July noticed their daughter messing about in the tree. "What in tarnation are you doing up there child?!" There was no reply forthcoming so he went inside with a couple of the grocery bags.

The others followed his example and soon enough Ernestine had all the help she could want. Something was not right though. What was it? The foul mood of her silent family? No, no...wait, she said to herself. Where was the youngest? Where was Josephine in all this? When she stopped to think of it Ernestine could not place where Josephine had been even hours before when she left for the store. After searching the house from top to bottom she could not find any trace of her youngest daughter. Stepping outside again she remembered Quadira sitting eerily in the tree, ignoring all that transpired on the ground. When Ernestine approached the girl continued to be preoccupied. "Quadira! You come down here right now. Where is Josephine at? We ain't seen her in hours!"

Instead of climbing down from her sanctuary Quadira simply smiled down on her family. "She in the Havenot House."

"Havenot House? Now what in creation is that?!"

"A good place," Quadira answered, happier now than she had been for days. "A place where she can't get hurt no more."

"Hurt no more? She ain't been hurt at all. Least not yet, not 'til I find that troublesome child. Now you come down here girl, you come down here this very instant."

Quadira sulked only a little bit after that exchange, the events of the day apparently enough to keep her spirits high on the way down to Earth. Ernestine lead the spacey girl back inside only to find another conflict brewing. It was July again.

"Hershel!" he screamed. "What...what in...I mean, what in God's holy name done happened here?!" He was holding an empty martini glass and shaking it furiously at the children. "It was you! Malcolm! Don't just stand there like you ain't done nothing boy. Come on out and admit it. Admit it! All right, fine then," he said. "Well that's it. Malcolm's going packin'."

This caught Ernestine off guard. "Now just what does that mean?"

"He can mooch off his uncle Charlie for all I care. That's where he's going."

"Charlie? *Charlie?* Uh-uh."

"*Uh-huh!*"

Ernestine snorted. "That no-good brother of yours? I wouldn't trust him with a dead dog, much less my only son."

"Now what in the world is *that* supposed to mean woman? A dead dog? Just what would somebody do with a dead dog anyhow? You tell me."

"Well now what sense are you making July? Not any from what I can tell."

He made some short dismissive gestures with his hands. “Malcolm, you go on up to your room and get some clothes together.”

“Oh no you don’t!” Ernestine told the boy. “You don’t leave your mother!”

Dee snickered at the scene from the sidelines while holding some ice to her neck. “Sending Malcolm away ain’t no kind of solution or nothing. He got his problems, sure, but he’s just a little part of the real problem.”

“Oh yeah?” July countered. “And just what might that be? Whycome you don’t just finish that thought and hip us all up to what’s goin’ on? Maybe it’s ‘cause you ain’t got nothing to say!”

“I’ll tell you what the *problem* is, I’ll tell you,” Dee assured him. “The problem is *this family*.”

Ernestine just could not sit by and listen to it any longer. “This family ain’t the problem. We love each other and get by fine. We’ll survive this little problem, yes we will child, you’ll see.”

A Serenade to Beauty Everlasting

"Now hatred is by far the longest pleasure!
Men love in haste, but they detest at leisure."
Lord Byron, *Don Juan*

...BY THAT TIME MY antagonized mind was bubbling with the lewdest of obscenities dredged up from the coarse sediment of my darkest sentiments, the delirium-inducing effects shaping my mind into little more than a pillory for the malformed husk of a bitch that she had become: yes, a pillory, because the very admonitions which had sprung from the well of her swelling animosity ensured that sleep was a laughable, contemptible, essentially repulsive notion. *Sleep. Sleep? Sleep! Yes...hmm...how ludicrously evil...argh*, I thought, yes, perhaps I *would* sleep, out of sheer spite if nothing else. What a third-world torturer it would make me to behave in such a callous manner, to sleep, to sleep the slumber of one enfeebled by the enormity of their own cruelty. Oh, the horrifying delights that flitted through the corridors of my consciousness in those moments! Oh! Preposterous! Precisely so because I knew full well of her awareness, yes, her very recognition of my overflowing contempt for even the slightest utterance belonging to her—a fact which thus ensured a remorseless and often inane cascade of babbling at all times; it was, in ridiculous fact, her very knowledge of my loathing which I hoped to exploit by sleeping. To lay there in silent comfort, recharging from the day's trifles, in resolute compliance with her command, would insult her to no end, surely, because she would know well enough that my only possible intention was to slap her in the face with vainglorious nonchalance, to provoke some revulsion in her, to disturb what miserable vestiges of rest may be left in her possession, to boldly say: "Here you beast, choke on this from now until kingdom come!" What a triumph it would be, to sleep! After the vicious tirade that had leapt well beyond human endurance—nay, human comprehension—even a host of the deceased would be hard pressed to lay still, much less allow themselves to recline into the sandman's embrace.

So it was decided; after well-nigh three quarters of an hour of internal debate and wrangling there was no other acceptable alternative than to simply stab my mate through the heart with my rancorous, obstinate urge to comply with her Draconian notions. Taking great care not to give the impression of being agitated I rolled onto my side, facing her so that I may fully gauge any forthcoming response. For minutes on end I lay still, my breathing in check, my eyes imperceptibly cracked to observe her reactions in the dark. Though I had to fight the urge to giggle in my childish contentment at having hatched such a scheme I somehow managed to maintain quiet. Soon enough, I promised myself, soon enough the imperious pillars supporting the facade of her tractable exterior would crumble under the assault of my silence, sending the whole thing crashing down onto the shoals of ignoble defeat. In the delirium brought on by that vision I was ravished by self-loathing, for as surely as I was utterly contemptible and godless I was equally—no, doubly—pleasured by my full enlightenment regarding my deeds, my contemplations, all of it. Oh yes, even malaria sufferers never had it that good! The fugue of scandalous wrath booming in the sarcophagus that my skull had become, it obscured every element from view, every memory and aspiration, leaving me adrift in the moment...the hateful moment! For each second that passed my passionate ire steeped in the cauldron of vengeance, to the boiling point, to the frothing point and beyond.

Perhaps a half hour had gone by since I set myself on that despicable course and still there was no reward to be had. She couldn't be asleep, no, so by default she had to be quite awake, fully aware of my vile actions, but still refusing to acknowledge me! How could it be that, after almost an hour and a half of laying in the bed, she had not attacked me like the vicious degenerate she was? The sheets were becoming damp, more than damp if the truth be told, as my metabolism must have been fluctuating wildly during the course of events in the sphere of my mind. Damp? No, such could not be the word to describe my condition at the time. It would be far better to say that the sheets had become saturated with the profusion of salty perspiration to the point of becoming not unlike the soaked strips of linen used for the purposes of mummification. With such thoughts swirling through my skull I began to thrash about madly, trapped in the cloth as I was, unable to escape and gagging on an abundance of saliva. Despite my exertions all I achieved was an entanglement which served to compress my chest and further deprive me of the ability to draw breath.

Before I knew what had transpired I found myself free of the sheets, gasping in the dark, feeling oddly uneasy as if the struggle itself had been something to live for, but being free of it I was left without meaning, without purpose. No, no, nonsense I told myself. I would still have my revenge, if nothing else! Though my skin cooled with rapidity at having its slathering of sweat exposed to the night air I began to roil inwardly once more. In the period that followed I put on the act of sleeping once again, surprised still that she had not responded to my earlier fit of "sleep" and especially that she had let my frenzy to escape entombment under the covers go unanswered.

I was once more on the path to pathological bedroom antics, having only been derailed momentarily. How I so desperately looked forward to her anguish! A vivacious epiphany filled my senses, depriving me of any warning that she was about to kick my leg under the covers. The ridiculous crone's palsied leg convulsed just then, her yellowed, fungus-ridden toenails digging into my skin without remorse. Afterwards she simply rolled away from me without a single word of apology! Now *that* offense, coupled with her obstinate and wholeheartedly malicious ignoring of my repeated affronts, could not be forgiven. Something had to be done, something drastic, even for me; retaliation, a demolishing retaliation, needed to be promptly launched her way.

In this state I rolled over onto my side, counted to the predetermined number one hundred forty-eight, and with only the faintest hint of altering my breathing I began to snore. It was exhilarating, this exercise, exacting my revenge in such a petty and low-minded manner. My steadfast conviction enabled me to ward off my body's natural desire to quicken the pace of my breaths in my excitement. No, with the force of my mind, driven on by senselessly brutal banality, I tightened the reins on my diaphragm, forced my belly to expand ever so slightly further with each passing breath, staggered the incoming air through the tangled miasma of my nasal cavity, and soon enough I was snoring wholeheartedly. Each repetition was so tedious, so pathetic in its intent, so grating to any within hearing, that the experience was bordering on erotic.

"Willard!" she shrieked in that raspy, tainted warble. "Will you please knock it off with this foolishness! We both know that you aren't sleeping, not with that preposterous snoring and grade-school attitude of yours—"

"Well I'm certainly not sleeping now—"

"—I know you Willard—"

"—am I? Am I?!" I intended to keep up the ruse no matter what. "How can I sleep—"

"—shut up you idiot! You think you're some kind of big-brain?"

Measuring my words I retorted with, "Confound your ill-temper you obtuse leper of a beast!"

"Well you aren't! You're nothing! *Nothing!*"

"A weasel's ejaculate is what you are intellectually, you hideous woman—"

"You're a cockroach, that's what you are! A cockroach in a man's body! Squirming around in that pasty shell of a man, making me want to puke all over the place!"

For some peculiar reason this shook my foundation in a special, not entirely unpleasant, way that sent me into paroxysms of indignant ecstasy as I clasped my hands around her wretched throat. "You witch! You insufferable exhorter of all that is repugnant and, and filthy and lecherous, and, and...you harlot!" Only for a moment was I at a lack of words. "Bloody pus from a turtle's hemorrhoid is what you are! Can you imagine?! Can you imagine?! What it must be like for me, laying here in this abominable tapeworm's den you call a house, next to a pus-filled skin sack such as yourself?! Do you know how it feels?! Damn it all, *I—am—a—genius*!"

Even in the blackness of the bedchamber I could discern the terrain of her face contorted not with fright but ignorant malice. "Get your hands off me you sick pervert! Get away...*away!* And go calculate in hell!"

"In hell? I've already been inside you, you insipid witch, and I've no intention of reliving that nauseating experience—"

"How dare you! *How—dare—you!*" She was madly clawing at my torso and seething incomprehensibly, her bellows alternating between the deepest guttural, raw, traumatized, animalistic tones and the shrilling of a savage being torn apart by machinery. This was the row at three in the morning. On neither of our minds at that time was my Nobel Prize acceptance speech, to be delivered that afternoon before a multitude of luminaries from the varying disciplines of the arts and sciences. Suddenly she found syllables again. "You blubbery piece of crap! You're not a man! You're not a man! You're not a man at all, you piece of crap!"

"Appolonia!" I howled directly into her unsanitary ear while throttling her with all the murderous intent at my disposal. "I shall finish you this time...yes! Yes!" I cried in full ecstasy. "You've pushed me too far you disgusting piece of human trash! Die! *Die!* I want you to be fully *aware* of your death, you devil's toadstool!"

But she would not go without a fight. The garbled cries my fingers trapped in her throat were not pleas for mercy, no, they were quite the contrary; Appolonia was undoubtedly paraphrasing my words to declare her own intents. With fingers warped into claws by the dementia she had been whipped into my wife gouged every available surface of my body, bloodying us both in the process, until our cries of anguish and fruitless, resonating disgust were indistinguishable.

"*Shut up!* You bunch of freakin' lunatics! Shut up! I'm trying to *sleep!*" came a voice from the room next door, accompanied by the pounding of fists against the plaster. Curse her...curse her for being slatternly, humpbacked—at least in my eyes—and above all else our daughter...Appolina.

"Shut that anus of a hole in your face," was my reply, rising in both pitch and volume by the end until the voice carrying it no longer sounded like my own, quavering and screeching as it was. Wildly I flung my fists at the wall during the interminable round of "Oh!"'s which followed, from both mother and daughter, out of unadulterated repulsion for the man they both should have been looking up to, should both have been lavishing admiration on. Was I ashamed of myself, of my despicable treatment of my family—my "loved ones"—my very willingness to sink to such depravities? Why...yes, indeed! However, this fact only served to spur me on to new heights of viciousness.

The words that followed were, for the most part, reiterations of the epitaphs that had already consumed the better part of our sleeping hours, Appolonia and I grappling and cursing while Appolina wailed laments and sobs at the boundaries of her voice's endurance next door. Around about 4:30 I launched into my "parasite" rant: "I have had my fill of the vermin I once embraced as a family, do you know that, do you *comprehend*, are you even *capable* of *comprehension* you worm? Day in and day out I have nothing to do but pry your toothy suckers off, you and that slavering thing you call a daughter, you're leeches! Both of you! You want no more out of life in your simple-minded hunger than to find a good man, search him out, and having found him you drool—don't deny it, I've seen you daily for thirty years—and you leap upon his guileless generosity, you throw yourself into the fathomless fountain of his tolerance, then drink it up, you suck him dry—*curse you Appolina are you listening, because you are no better*—you drain his essential juices dry, rip the very lifeblood from his veins, until there is nothing left, nothing left, nothing at all for the man who gave everything! I am assailed on all sides by lampray-minded creatures, yes, well I'll tell you: I shall suffer it no more! No more will my spleen fester under your assault you spineless invertebrate pagans! Once I was a softhearted man, naive to the world's wickedness! But you! *You!* I've watched in horror as you have, as you have wormed, yes, as you've wormed your way under my skin, wriggling through my veins, until you eventually struck my heart! My precious heart! And tainted it, yes, that's what you have done, with your insidious ways, infected me with your slithering, convoluted, demoralized leech's spirits. Well now! I know the solution when it comes to dealing with leeches. I'm an educated man. *Fire!* Yes, fire, hear the word and tremble knowing that I will burn you away with Prometheus' deadly gift, you worms, you slimy worms, nematodes and whores, you'll all burn! Where is my lighter?! Where is my lighter I say?! Before this night is through I swear this tapeworm's den will burn to the ground, burn to the ground and beyond, burn to the very depths of Hades! That's right, yes, Hades! The place that spawned you. Make your final peace with whatever pagan invertebrate gods you worship, you—"

"*Sleep!*" fired Appolonia, in octaves which I had not heard exiting a human before, in what was more a siren of discontent than a voice. "*Sleep! Why—won't—you—just—slee-ee-ee-eep!!!*"

"Because I," I found myself screaming, now bolt upright in the bed with a profusion of sweat and saliva on my lips and an indignant finger in the air, without (to my horror) the slightest clue as to what I may say, "I am the divine Willard! I am he, he who by providence—*no!!* Not by God's decree, *no*, but by my *own* decree, by my *own* self-determination, by all that is holy, in total and final *revulsion* at the *thought* of all the foul-mouthed corseted *whores*, the overwhelming *reek of dog urine* pervading the world and undermining the *stability* of my *liver functions*, by—"

Suddenly an otherworldly sonic horror the likes of which has not been heard before or since unleashed itself in Appolina's room, a sound presumably organic in nature, a sound capable of spoiling even that which could rot no further, a sound capable of depriving all the saints of their virtues and of causing the angels to rain from heaven's heights dead from brain aneurysms, a sound capable of even causing

Appolonia and I to pause our wallowing momentarily. Following the duration of this outburst, when I managed to force my hands away from my ears, I could hear the outraged glass settling in a carpet of shards throughout the household, and from above a fine dusting of plaster drifted down choking our inflamed respiratory systems.

My head still numb from hours of rampaging I threw back the covers and slid out of bed. The thought festered in my mind that I must root out the source of that sanguine sound. "Appolonia," I whispered, but for some reason my whisper was tiny, too small, and not due to the level of my voice. This troubled me deeply and I couldn't tell if my wife had responded, so again I whispered, "Appolonia," but despite the fact that my second utterance was more emphatic it reached scarcely deeper into my ears than the first. Then I realized what had befallen me: an unnatural ringing which dwelled somewhere in the background, reverberations of the sound perhaps, which partially obscured normal tones, the sound had latched onto my ears with a horrible ferocity. "*Appolonia!*" I bellowed, throwing myself down on top of her with all of my might, not caring that the bulk of my frame would snap the diminished little twigs that served as her arms and legs. A shock of sorts rattled me when I felt my weight crushing nothing more than the mattress itself. "What...what has become of you?!" I said, my hands sweeping the bed in their search for her.

Insolent, wretched light exploded my pupils suddenly. "I'm right here you idiot! What the devil are you doing anyway?!" She aimed the cursed flashlight directly at my face, into my eyes, intentionally, curse her.

"Will you—" I grunted, squinting painfully, attempting to wave away the beam of brightness. "Will you lower that thing?!"

"What? This?" She stepped closer, aiming the flashlight at my face with both hands, jiggling the thing back and forth to be all the more aggravating.

"Woman, I warn you—"

"Oh yeah? What? What are you going to do about it you rotten old bastard!"

"Let that be your death sentence you hoary old harpy!" I shouted in response, lunging forward. In my haste I miscalculated the distance between us and fell short, directly onto the unyielding floor. Pounding my fist on that very floor, with her laughing above me, and that hellish ringing in my ears, well that was too much for me to bear, for any man of conscience to bear, and as a man of honor—extolled, unquestioned honor—I swore a revenge that would shock even the devils themselves. Clutching, rending her nightgown with my straining hands I shouted, "I am an astronomer...a poet...an educator! I demand the respect—"

"Get away!" Appolonia shrieked, blasting me once more with the flashlight. My threat of fire, cleansing fire, came back to me then. "Like I don't have enough to worry about without you being a pompous ass. What was that horrible sound?!"

"That sound..." So soon I had managed to forget. Yes, that sound, the sound which had inflicted itself upon my ears, my innocent ears, hellfire and balderdash, yes, I would seek out the source of that sound and have my revenge! "Appolina's room..." I found myself unable to release the beast's clothing when she attempted to move away. The sinews, the skin, all of it, the whole of my body was wrecked from the night's exertions.

"Get off of me! Get off of me! We have to see if our daughter's okay and here you are groveling and being petty as always and for God's sake Willard won't you just grow up and get off me you vicious dog GET AWAY—" and then her feet began to rain an executioner's storm on my shoulders, my head, my ribs and back and arms, until she sent herself tumbling to the floor in her vigor. A sharp cry of pain from Appolonia was the only sound in the household, followed by light sobs...and that murderous ringing!

"Fine then," I screamed. "Forget me, forget your husband, rush to your daughter's side why don't you," still screaming, still clutching at her while she dragged herself along the floor, both of us crawling and grappling and barking into the hallway of that Swedish villa, sweating, bleeding still, grimy from my skin to my soul, cursing the day I ever met Appolonia, cursing the day I moved the family to Sweden in anticipation of the recognition I deserved—the Nobel Prize in literature—dragging ourselves to the door of our daughter's bedroom, and Appolonia unable to reach the doorknob because my hands and arms were wrapped so tightly around her, my hatred being in heat at that moment.

After a series of unintelligible cries and devilish gougings Appolonia drove me off. Even so she was not fast enough to lock me out. An incredible match of wills ensued, she on the inside of our daughter's room attempting to seal the door and I on the outside growling, roaring, focusing the whole of my strength on the task of gaining entry. "Just let me check on my precious one," Appolonia wailed. "She needs me!"

"*I'm not stopping you! I'm not stopping you! I'm not stopping you!*"

"Yes you are!"

"No I'm not!"

"She could be dead and here you are behaving like a monster!"

"Don't think that we could ever be so lucky! That mongrel! That whore! That humpbacked, slatternly—"

"*Silence!*"

"*No!*"

"I won't let you in here! You'll be the death of us all!"

At length I launched the piece of wood off its hinges and sent Appolonia flying into a dresser of some sort. A hail of trinkets and collegiate texts leapt from the dresser while I howled triumphantly. "You malignant torturers! Here I am! Here I am! Come greet me with your claws and fangs and bloodsucking ways!" When I was met only by silence in the dark I threw the light switch to the "on" position with such violence that it was ripped from its mounting. What first drew my attention was the state of the wall directly behind Appolina's headboard. The confounded creature had been pounding on the plaster with such vehemence during our turmoil that what had been a perfectly good and decent wall had become cracked, riddled with imperfections, just like Appolina herself. "Appolina! What is the meaning of this?!" I spewed while rushing to finger the wall in my concern. "Have you any inkling just how much work it will take to repair this? Have you? I don't suppose you will be the one to labor away on it, will you? Will you? No, no, I think not, you mangy sloth. Yes, this will have to come out of your pocket, at the very least..."

When I turned to the bed which I knew her to be resting on I was surprised to find that every word I had spoken had been ignored with spite, with the most devious of pathological apathy, by mother and daughter alike. Appolina lay upon the twisted bedding, disheveled, her fingers bent into claws at the ends of her limp arms, the length of her auburn hair splayed about the pillows and sheets like vines strangling a tomb, with no indication of breathing easily discernible, nor any sign of consciousness. Appolonia was edging forward on her elbows, desperate, holding back tears, eyes fixed on her daughter.

"Appolina?" she beckoned. "Appolina? Darling?"

"'Darling'?! Rubbish! What spell has this witch cast over you, woman? Have you or have you not noticed the condition of this wall?! Just look at it! Ruined! How are we to entertain the members of society who will undoubtedly call on us, or the vast sea of journalists who will line up to interview me?!"

"*Appolina?*" Appolonia was struggling onto the mattress, clutching her daughter's leg and shaking it in some ignorant attempt at reviving her.

"Oh. Very well then. Ignore the wall, ignore me. Will you do me that courtesy? Would you do your husband the courtesy of ignoring him? I implore you."

Without paying me any mind she continued her ascent until she was fully on the bed. Shaking Appolina by the shoulders she cried, "Wake up! Wake up! Answer me!" With no response forthcoming Appolonia finally turned to me, saying, "Willard! She won't wake up! What if she's...what if she's—"

"Out of my way!" I bellowed, shoving her to the side. "Listen to your father! I demand that you drop this charade this very instant and answer for your transgressions against this house!" Appolina's head lolled from side to side as I lifted her from the bed. A cursory examination revealed both a pulse and soft breathing. "Wake! I command you! Rise!" Soon enough my hands were raining slap after thunderous slap across her unresponsive face. "It's what you deserve! It's what you deserve for that horrible shrieking! You've ruined my night, you've ruined my sleep, you—"

"Stop it Willard!" Appolonia hollered, while doing her best to restrain me. "Just stop it, stop it, stop it, stop—"

With a mighty shrug of my shoulders I shouted, "Unhand me woman!" but my efforts failed to dislodge the cloying creature. "Unhand me! Don't touch her! Don't you touch her!" It was only a simple matter of course that she would instantly lunge for Appolina no sooner than the warning had passed my lips. The fracas that followed is a blur in my mind now but I do recall a turtle, a small snapping turtle I believe, that much is certain. Regardless, Appolina never showed signs of awareness during the terrible strife which consumed the next half hour. Neither my wife nor I were able to rouse her, or our own sensibilities, our senses of self respect or decency. The fact that she doted so on our daughter caught on my thoughts as a great white would snare on a boogie-boarder, mangling my sense of perspective in the process, deforming what I know on normal occasions to be a reasonable and virtuous mind. "What is wrong with you?!" I queried repeatedly and, receiving no intelligible answer, began to foam at the mouth.

"Just leave us alone! You monster! Just leave us be," was my wife's mantra during this time, or was it? Oh, I suppose it doesn't matter now exactly what it was that she said; the sentiment behind the words is correct for her mood at the time.

Still rankled by the piercing sound coating my ears with its syrupy burning I yanked the wedding band from my ring finger. "Fine then! Fine! You like her so much do you?! Why don't you just marry her then! Ha, that's right, who needs me, who the devil needs a genius like me around when they have a perfectly good sap to waste their time away?!" A veritable Niagara Falls of admonitions and epithets poured forth from Appolonia's mouth then, flooding my consciousness with its swirling, muddied message, a sharp undertide threatening to suck me under. But no! I stood fast, anchored in my savage, rapturous hatred. "Go on," said I, "really, I insist! Marry her you fiend! She's the only beast hideous enough to deserve the torment of a life with you!" So saying I thrust my wedding band upon Appolina's ring finger and hurled my wife to the mattress. "I now pronounce you beast and fiend! You can stay in here from now on! I have had my fill! No longer will we share a room, a roof perhaps, but I'll no longer suffer sharing a room with you!" Spinning on my heel I rushed to the doorway, buoyant now on a surprising feeling of elation at the thought of having the entire bedroom to myself, to do with as I please, being able to sleep for as long or as little as I wished without having to wake to the repugnant death mask that was Appolonia's face.

Just as quickly as it had been born inside me the happiness was vanquished by a perilous notion, a gut-wrenching feeling, a gruesome suspicion. Within a moment's time I raced back to the bed where my wife lay sobbing and grabbed hold of her wrist, having thought the matter over and concluding that I could not trust the two of them alone. Who knows what they may get up to? The risk was incalculable. All that I had worked for, the myriad successes I had accrued in my years, it could all be lost by this one careless action. Troubled further by the thought that the incessant, relentless debacle had grown quite tiresome to all concerned I dragged Appolonia kicking and screaming back to our bedroom, then changed my mind at the precipice, deciding it would be better for her to sleep on the sofa, or in the back yard perhaps.

"Are you insane?!" she shrieked on hearing my request. Acting more quickly than my sleep-deprived mind could fathom Appolonia wriggled free of my grasp and soundly slammed the door, locking it. That was it; no debate, no struggle. Just like that! Bruised and battered, unrecognizable as the man I had once considered myself to be, feeling a fathomless inertia threatening to send me spiraling out of my course, I felt my shoulders sink as the faithless anger drained away, leaving me friendless in a world of enemies. Her reproachments continued, crawling out from behind the safety of the door, but they were unable to take hold of me for I was slipping away, deep into the recesses of my mind. Who can truly say just how long it was that I stood there enveloped by that borderless, hazy torpor? I came to after some time and realized that all was quiet in the house once again.

Taking a look about at my opulent surroundings I felt a familiar scribbling and scratching inside my skull: a plan was hatching. Yes, a plan, one which I allowed my animosity to nurture, which in turn gave the plan a profound strength, an abundant strength, enough strength to lend some to my malnourished madness. which in turn returned it to its former glory. Without a care for what may come I made my way down to the rear door as quickly as I could in my diminished physical capacity. When my hands were upon the door itself I viewed the carnage wrought by the shrill scream that had its way with the household earlier in the night. The glass from the small window in the door lay at my feet, hopelessly shattered, waiting to slice my skin if given the chance. All at once I came to recognize just how desperately cold it had grown in our home, how entirely frigid and devoid of the warmth associated with life, and suddenly found myself spitting in contempt of the thought, of myself, of any and every thing.

"Bah! Rubbish! *Silly talk!*" I said, stomping the very mound of glass itself in my anger. Despite the sobering pain screaming its way through my body I stomped upon the glass time and time again, hopping up and down on it as a child in the throes of tantrum would, further breaking it down into ridiculously small and sharp bits, flattening the mound and dispersing the glass until I was gasping for breath from the combined burden of my pain and exertion. No matter, I told myself. "No matter! To Hades with hellfire and harlots!" I snarled, no longer caring what I was saying, as long as it was vicious enough to embolden me, to bolster the resolve which may flag in the presence of skin made into no more than a loose mesh by shards of glass. "To hell with Hades!" was my quiet battle cry as I launched myself out the door into the freeze-dried air. After all, quietness was key to the plan if it was to be executed with any success. True, I had been jumping up and down on breaking glass with all my weight but surely that wouldn't have caused enough noise to tip Appolonia off to my activities.

With my lungs scorched by the deep-space atmosphere and my skin already growing numb, my eyes running in the attempt to compensate for the air totally devoid of moisture, and the tears instantly freezing on my cheeks, I trod across the back yard as carefully as possible. The hardened earth itself seemed every bit as malicious as the glass still embedded in my feet. With every trepidatious tread my grunting grew louder, ever louder, as I stealthily made my way to the latticework. Arriving at the base of the decorative crap I ascended its heights, guided by the rays of the dawn, with the expertise of a cat burglar, only shrieking with all my heart and soul at the mind-searing pain ever so slightly, though not enough to alert Appolonia I assured myself. When finally I did reach the second level of the house, directly at the window of our bedroom, I was vindicated by the darkness within. *Back to your black lair*, I told my self-doubt, *flee from my victorious return to the bed which is rightfully mine, yes, a return worthy of MacArthur, or whoever that accursed general was, Patten, Grant, Lee, the Desert Fox—that German, whoever he was—Van Helsing or whatever*; only I was Pretorious! I shall return! Willard Pretorious! Or, as I would be remembered by future generations, Victorious Pretorious!

At precisely the moment that thought bombarded my mind the pain of a broomstick striking my face bombarded through my senses. Somehow I managed to keep from falling to my death then, quite possible only due to the fact that my unfortunate fingers and tortured feet were caught and tangled in that fragile latticework which—bless its preposterous wooden frame—held fast under the burden of my terrified weight.

"Go away Willard!" the harridan squawked. "Get down from there before you kill yourself!"

"I'll not be the one to perish in this conflict you unfit beast of burden—my burden—I'll—" and without notice the end of the broom struck my face, the harsh bristles scouring my face as it was in fact not the broom I had thought it to be, but was instead that cursed besom made of twigs and twine.

"I'm warning you! Get down from there! Do you want the neighbors to see this?! I'm warning you," she yelled, emphasizing her words with another smack of the besom.

With her words I could feel the induration of my heart accelerating, finalizing, becoming a permanent feature. "You'll not assault my person with that piece of trash again you witch!" I cried, desperately grabbing the handle. A magnificent tug-of-war followed which resulted in much profanity and the cumulative force of our struggles repulsing us in equal measure, she being flung back into the depths of that hookworm's paradise and I left to cling with the diminishing hope of maintaining my position on the side of our house. Reminding myself that I was none other than Victorious Pretorious, I labored diligently and did finally take hold—flesh-penetrating hold—on the jagged window frame. With my last reserves of energy I heaved myself through the empty window, up to my chest, when a strange odor and burst of hot air rushed against me.

Before I could realize what she was doing Appolonia brandished the now-flaming besom against my crown, setting my hair alight in the process! Utter, despicable, pulse-quickening pandemonium followed, during which my swine of a wife ran around in circles screaming at the top of her lungs, and I dragged the length of my body over the slivers of glass in the window frame, not feeling a thing as all my horror was focused on the inferno raging across my scalp. Launched through the air in my frenzy I toppled onto the bed awkwardly, injuring my shoulder in the process. In my frantic thrashings I did not perceive just how

Appolonia dealt with the flaming besom, but I did extinguish the flames on my head by burrowing and spinning, burrowing and spinning, like a mole or shrew trapped in a collapsing tunnel which was quickly becoming its tomb. After assuring myself that the flames had been vanquished I sat up, the sheets forming a grotesquely distorted turban that was huge and painful on my tender head.

We stared at each other in the darkness briefly, our eyes again growing accustom to the lack of light, before she uttered, "I want you out of here." With my breaths still too labored to reply she again took the initiative. "I want you out. Gone. Out of here, out of this room, out of this house! Willard! Do you hear me?!"

Finding my store of bitterness depleted I could only say, "I want to sleep."

"Well I don't *care*—"

"I only want to *sleep!*"

"I don't *care* if you want to sleep!"

"Just let me sleep woman! This is all that I ask! No more of this abominable row, I've had my fill of it all. I just want to rest." With undue force I flopped on the bed several times, attempting to become comfortable, discovering that the bed had grown as cold and hard as the general atmosphere.

"If this is another of your tricks—"

"Oh, this is no ruse, I just need some sleep, no matter how insignificant, I need my sleep. Tomorrow is my day of days after all. Are you trying to ruin it in advance?!"

"No. No! Go ahead and sleep then if it's so important."

"Well it is." I sighed with alacrity as my frustration mounted.

Finally Appolonia slipped into bed next to me. What seemed a long silence passed, the darkness doing the opposite of humming, becoming absorptive, like an acoustically treated chamber, making me feel all the more isolated. "*I told you to just go to sleep to begin with!*" she rasped before finally assailing the cluster of bedding trapping my head.

"Will you leave that be?! When you pull on it my head hurts!"

"Well I need some sheets—"

"No!" I said, attempting to pin the cloth to my head, but in the end this effort was short lived due to the severe pains trotting over my scalp, assisting Appolonia in her efforts. After losing this skirmish I lay stock still, the pillow in revolt under my neck, the scratches caused by the besom stinging and tingling oddly, my feet raw and sticky causing the covers to cling to them, the bleeding from the cuts on my palms seeming to subside, the clawing and biting from earlier in the night an affront to my serenity. True, I would have been placid at the time if not for the wounds which had converted me into a relief map of pathos, yes, I would be the picture of saintly bliss if not for that demoness!

"Good Lord Willard, you smell like roasted hot dogs!" she cried, smacking her lips with disdain.

Through gritted teeth I slowly, clearly, painfully enunciated: "*I just want to sleep.*"

"Well then *just sleep.*"

"I would if you could find it in your indecent self to restrain that flapping maw of yours..."

"Oh! I knew you just came back in here to quarrel! That's it!"

"I—"

"That's it! Get out!"

"*I'm trying to sleep! I'm trying to sleep! I'm trying to sleep!*" On and on we went until my innards were churning as if in some fiendish butter churning device contrived by the archfiend himself, twisting and knotting, depriving me any even the faintest physical comfort. Somehow the nauseating trail of offensive verbiage tapered to a vanishing point and we were alone in the dark once more, no longer sharing the room, the bed, our hatred, only projecting ourselves inward, searching out some peaceful region in which to reside whilst our bodies shut down. This was without a doubt the most difficult stumbling point of the entire sordid night. Soon enough the trials of the long suffering night hours bore down on my mind and spirit until I had been pressed down into my subconscious mind, flirting with a weak dream state as I drifted in and out of wakefulness. A shocking discovery awaited me when I woke: the convoluted disappointments of my family had been cast off by angry porters during my travels. The men gave me vivid descriptions of my family's cries rising from the water as our ship left them in its wake, never to be heard from again. The audacity of the men shocked me as I had not been consulted first, nor had I even been allowed the chance to view the event myself. Nevertheless we soon made port in a Persian harbor, and all manner of finery was bestowed upon me on arrival. A mouthwatering and tempting array of exotic fruits, meats, and other savories were laid out by a parade of handsomely dressed men who spoke no English, but I refrained from cursing their ignorance. The Sultan of the land was brought to greet me personally in a caravan of gilded gold sedan chairs shouldered by a horde of ferocious men. The Sultan spoke to me in humble tones praising his pagan deities for the glorious appearance of one so endowed with intellect. Furthermore, he begged me to stay and teach his people the path to righteousness, modern intellectual righteousness, and—despite the urge to bite his nose severely—I accepted his offer. I was given the grand tour of his kingdom during a festival of welcome that lasted forty days and forty nights, and after a whirlwind immersion in delicacy after delicacy I found myself situated in a magnificent palace that defies the descriptions afforded by Western tongues. I admit it was all phantasmal in truth, but I believed that I was an ambassador of intellect in this strange land. During my stay I was befriended by many persons of every race and sex, bonded with them, formed the kind of relations that I did not know were possible: open, trusting friendships where anything may be discussed, anything may be revealed, and mutual appreciation and gratitude flowed as freely as breath between us. Fellowship! The joys of fellowship that had eluded me my whole life long were at last revealed to me. The kindness of strangers...why, yes! It did exist! That, and much more.

Not only did the finest jewels and clothes adorning me but in my haunted state I believed earnestly that I did in fact have a harem of bodacious buxom beauties culled from the New York avant-funk intelligentsia at my disposal to indulge any whim, no matter how trivial, such as researching how many times the word "forlorn" was mentioned in *The Rockford Files* television series. The fact was that I had two avant-funk feminist models working on that very task, I was sure, and wielding such substantial authority, the mere thought of it caused slippery giggles to bubble up from the reservoirs of my subconscious. The untroubled sounds loomed all too loud in my ears and threatened to wake me from the magical reverie blessing my tortured mind. No, no, I allowed myself to recede into the mists of hope and again immersed myself in a world where I was lounging in Roman garb on a bed of powdered gold, while a scantily and retro clad Brooklyn-born hipster socialite—a Jewish Puerto Rican brunette I do believe—was dropping delectable chunks of kipper into my waiting mouth. Ha-ha! What a life it would be! They gathered around—forty in all—anxious and pleased beyond reason to hear my sage words, to hang with rapt attention on every syllable I might deem suitable for them to bear witness to. I proceeded to expound on the need for a more caring sociopolitical system, about the need for networks of concerned citizens to reach out to the challenged, to at-risk youths, to empower the disenfranchised, et cetera, and to a woman they all nodded at the appropriate times, even breaking into applause when they became overcome by their own enthusiasm. Standing on the arched backs of two who had fought others away for the opportunity to support my weight I stood above my adoring horde, each of them clamoring for my attention, assuring me that I was still the man I had been in my youth, assuring me that I was an intellectual juggernaut the likes of which this world has never come close to contemplating, epochal in proportions. No, these were not wenches who lived only to pilfer my vault of peerless consideration and generosity, to siphon my tolerance and stab me in the back...no! These were *women*, true and honest women, examples of femininity as I deserved to know them. Not only that, but after my delivery of the important message of brotherly love and compassion the most beautiful, wonderful secret in all creation was revealed to me by God—God who had been watching my whole life long, waiting for the moment that I achieved total and final enlightenment, God who had been so moved by my speech—and the final, most exhilarating secret of all existence was—

"Willard you're a fool and a lout and a bastard! You *id*iot! I've woken you up three times and three times you've gone back to sleep! And now what?! And now what?! Well, I'll tell you! We're running late!" Appolonia had to decimate my slumber just as the pinnacle of supreme cosmic consciousness was in the process of being revealed to me. Impaled by her freakish voice and stabbed through my brain by the sun's millions of dagger-like rays I had no need for a pillow being slammed across my chest, but Appolonia disagreed.

Attempting to fend off the light, the horrid light, and the lumpy, lice-infested piece of waste that Appolonia called a pillow, I tried to raise my hands but found that they—in accordance with the rest of my upper body's attitude—were painfully resistant. Troubled by the ringing which swirled at the periphery of my hearing I leapt from the bed with undue vigor ready to settle things once and for all. As soon as I did so I found myself screaming at the unwelcome sensations flaring like a distress signal from the forgotten wounds of my feet. Teetering for long moments, struggling not to fall and hurt myself, I swung my arms wildly, frightened sounds escaping me, my hips swaying and knees jumping from side to side without rhyme or reason. On seeing this Appolonia cackled a horrid, cold crone's cackle which registered 9.0 on the Pretorious Hatred Scale, so enraging me that I toppled instantly. The fall served to further aggravate the shoulder I had injured in my fall from the window after ascending the latticework. I tried to form some arrangement of words that would assault her as surely as fists, but in my heightened state of nervous emotional congestion, in which anger and sadness, exhilaration and awe all sang equally loud, buzzing like the flies trapped in a tomb after feasting on the dead, I found that the rush of thoughts and emotions created the equivalent of a train wreck in my mouth. *And still she cackled!*

Unable to conjure up any other place in the home where I might find immediate solitude I rushed to my private walk-in closet and locked it from the inside. After placing towels along the bottom edge of the door to muffle the sounds of the beast roaming free in the bedroom I recovered my light tools, among which were tweezers and a number of sharp instruments. While she did whatever it was that she did to try and make her Gorgon's head presentable, I worked at removing the multitude of impious glass shards—the devil's very progeny if ever he did procreate—a task that consumed the whole of the time allotted for my preparations. Looking at my wristwatch I felt my innards once more committing to insurrection, initiating a monstrous squirming and spastic, full-bodied revenge for a night of infamy. Before I could remedy the situation there was a sharp rapping at the closet door.

"Stop hiding in there and get some coffee for God's sake, wash up, do *something* at least. We're going to be late!"

"Oh, I *know* that already."

"Then why don't you do something about it? Well? We're going to be late. We're going to be late!"

"Who are you, the town crier?"

"No, are you the village idiot?"

"Oh ha, jolly good, oh so very clever Appolonia. I'm terribly wounded by that one, don't you know. Please, be a dear and call an ambulance, I fear for my cessation after being exposed to such incendiary wit."

"I'll expose you to more than just my wit you big dummy, now come out of there before you really do need an ambulance!"

Upon hearing this demand I ripped away whatever amount of clothing I had pulled on and charged out of the closet suddenly, stark naked, knocking my wife to the bed. She lay there stunned while I sped around the room in a circle, a bloody circle, my pain driving me on like a horse under its master's whip.

Appolonia stood and said, "We are going to be *late*, Willard, what don't you understand about this concept, you fool!"

"And what do I care for the time of dullards?! Let it be wasted, let every one of their seconds be cast to the depths of hell!"

"But what about the trustees, Willard?! The trustees will be there you cretin!"

"The trustees?! The trustees?!?" I frenzied with spittle, froth, and perhaps even blood accompanying with each vile syllable. "The Trustees can masturbate to death in a cauldron of boiling swine vomit–"

"Oh must you?!" she spat, again interrupting me with the plague that is her voice. "Must you be...*yourself*, on today of all days!"

Clawing at the very air I shouted, "It is my day you fiend, my day, *mine and mine alone*, may the devil take you!" At that time I was aware of the fact that my voice was weakening considerably, my vocal cords taut from exhaustion and a marathon of seething misuse. But, despite this knowledge, I simply could not help myself...or, I should say, I could only help myself to yet another serving of venom. "Curse this infernal ringing! You demons! You hell executioners!" My innards still writhing, now accompanied by my limbs and torso, I found that I was throwing myself into the furniture, into the walls, into the bedposts and finally to the floor, all the while uttering non-sensical abuses of the voice.

"Stop it! Stop it!" my wife screamed, hurling my collection of antique snuff containers at my twitching body until, overcome by a blasphemous urge, I leapt to my feet, pieces of ceramic embedded in me, and lunged at her in what had become our morning ritual to prepare for the day. "Mommy! Mommy!"

"Oh, disgusting! Not now Willard!" We grappled until she held me fast in a headlock of sorts and we sank to the floor in this arrangement, together, I still muttering "Mommy" and she still grunting "not now, not now" as I groped her malformed body until we were rolling around on the floor, on my devastated collection of precious snuff containers. "You fool! You'll ruin my dress!" she said. Despite the content of the words she was kissing me...and biting, it's true, biting me but also there were a fair number of kisses present in the mix. This is how we came to be wrapped around each other, disheveled and maddened with spiteful lust, when...

Appolina—wretched, unrepentant daughter of regret—opened the door in that instant and stood staring down on us. She was fully dressed in what can only be described as an impeccable arrangement for the day ahead. The stern glare of her emerald eyes, the cold radiance of her angelic skin, the dour purse of her full lips, it all seemed rather imposing in the light of day, coupled with our state when she flung the door open on us, the mongrel. The set of her strong jaw evinced the lifetime of malignancy that we had nurtured as a family...well, that they had nurtured I should say, as I was mostly the victim of their foul plots and no more a participant than that. "I'm ready and waiting to go to your special event, but if you can't be bothered with it I've got some friends who wanted to go to the pub."

"Oh—" I began, not knowing what retort may leap from my mouth.

No, she wouldn't have any discussion of the matter. "And do have the courtesy to at least put some clothing on, will you? I'll be scarred for life as it is." With that she slammed the door.

"I am *not* finished talking to you, young woman! Come back here and listen to your father!"

"Willard, leave her be," Appolonia pleaded.

"Begone!" I shouted, throwing her away from me. When I heaved the door open, my index finger prepared for a magnificent lecture, I was startled by the complete absence of my daughter. She was not to be found in either the hall or her bedroom.

"Even if you have no sense of shame put some clothes on Willard, in the name of decency!"

"Decency?! Decency?! We'll see just what is indecent! Now Appolina, you come back here!" With nothing more in my mind than to put that upstart in her place I raced toward the foyer, in agony, pale and naked and sweaty with patches of coarse hair scattered over my loose skin. I was sure the whelp had made her way to the foyer because I could hear her shoes on the floor. At the top of my lungs I shouted, "Listen to me when I say this, you ignorant beast, that pubs are the dens of low-witted, corseted whores and cow-patty sniffing, psychotic, armpit-licking fiends who engage in every act of depravity—" In the middle of my tirade I bounded around the corner of the stairs, ready to launch myself down them and scream directly into Appolonia's daughter's face, yes, save for the fact that I had found her to be with three of her college friends.

It is true: that handsome young scoundrel was present, the athletic one, a brattish child of some US armed forces flunky, accompanied by two girlfriends of Appolina's...one of which, much to my dismay, was that luscious model who always made my skin crawl like a submissive at the foot of a dominatrix. The swine! They stood gaping, their witless gawking inspiring only the most vile of thoughts in my mind, the most vicious emotions in my heart, lubricating the gears of malice. Even Appolina was, for once, stunned silent so I rushed to take advantage of her fatal hesitation.

"What?!" I shouted. "Have you no shame, staring at a naked man in his own home! Or is that it, perhaps you have never seen an actual man before!"

"Father! Go away! These are my friends!"

"I know well enough who these freaks are, these perverts! Well! You'll never catch me in a pub, you peeping toms! You voyeurs! I'll have you arrested, you malingerers!"

"*Father!*"

"This is my home, a man's home is his castle I say! I'll do as I please," I ranted, doing the raunchiest jumping jacks that my body could manage in its condition.

"Oh my God, I so don't need to see this," the model said, hiding behind her hands. "I'm sorry but I've got to split."

"Split?!" I raved, jumping ever more spastically. "I'll show you a split the likes of which you've never seen you harlots!" I cackled at the naked repulsion they exhibited. "Go back and dance for the pocket change of migrant workers in the States you nitwits! Ha-ha—" and then...I slipped on that foul throw rug which I had just the day before *insisted* Appolonia remove, for safety's sake. A tenaciously awful crashing and bumping ensued as I twisted and flopped down to the landing, demolishing the antique stand and vase before careening down the rest of the stairs. Although I still had life in me I felt as though my injured shoulder had been wrenched away by devils. I remained painfully conscious the whole time. Looking up I found myself surrounded by those whom only seconds earlier I had been profaning with every fiber of my being. They were all crowded over me, seemingly...concerned! How dejecting the thought was to me, how entirely shameful, that they should pity me or, worse still, wish to assist me even after I had attacked them like a swarm of rabid vermin. It became too much to bear, even for me, and I sprang to an upright position, enough so that I could turn and flee the scene. My retreat up the lonely staircase was somewhat clumsy in its execution as speed was a necessity.

"My God..." one of them gasped behind me in the foyer.

"Obviously he's quite ill...we're so sorry," the army brat managed to drool.

"Jesus, doesn't he know how to wipe?" one of them asked, watching my ascension with what one could only acknowledge as disgust.

Reaching the top I hurried around the corner and caught my breath, out of sight of my daughter and her heinous, lovely friends, while I could only clutch my throbbing shoulder and marshal my mental faculties for an attempt to restrain the tears. After minutes of general shaking and twitching and listening to those diabolic buffoons cajoling Appolina I found my legs were carrying me back the bedroom.

My wife was inside, sitting patiently on the bed, the remnants of my snuff containers still polluting the floor. Wordlessly I went about preparing for the day.

Finally Appolonia sighed and spoke aloud. "So you don't care about the trustees. So what. I can *live* with that. But Willard, you are aware, of course, that the prize is handed out by the King of Sweden himself!"

"Of course I am aware of that, how could I not be?!"

"It is just that you are going to make the King wait for you like some fool, that's all..."

"Oh, then, I suppose he will wait, now won't he. That's right *darling*, I am the man on whom kings wait hand and foot. Ha ha!" Just then Appolina burst in, running straight up to me, ramming herself boldly into me, standing chest to chest as though she had not one ounce of fear for me in her body. Just standing there, staring as she was, the whole thing was unnerving. To conceal this I spewed, "What in the world is wrong with you?! Bursting in on your father while he is dressing! I haven't even put my shirt on yet—"

"Shut up. Number one: I will not tolerate your behavior any more. Number two: if we have guests in the home and you go off into one of your fits again I'll stab you." She pulled a knife out of her dress then, for dramatic effect I am sure. "Number three: *why the hell is your wedding band on my finger?!*"

"Do not speak to your father in such a tone young woman."

"*I can't get it off!*" She said, struggling with the ring.

"What manner of idiot are you? A mere ring outstrips your ability to reason? Let me at it!" After knocking her other hand away I sought to remove the wedding band—which was, in fact, cemented in place—but Appolina swung the knife, forcing me back. A stare down followed, and all the while Appolonia sat on the bed, silent, unmoved by the events. Incapable of any other thought, any other words, a whisper slithered out of my mouth: "Oh, how I do hate you..."

Appolina snickered contemptuously "'Hatred is like fire—it makes even light rubbish deadly.' That's from *Janet's Repentance*. I doubt you've read it, as evidenced by the full night of rubbish you spouted, although you are the only one to be burned by it so far. And as for this," she said, holding up her hand to display the ring, "I'll get you for this."

"You don't get *me* with that ring, you get your *mother*, you beast." My words had no effect though. She was already out of earshot by the time I finished the sentence.

With that scene finished I went about completing my morning ritual. Appolonia was rattling on about something the entire time, something I refused to pay even the slightest attention to as I cleaned my wounds and washed and groomed myself. In the end I found it to be wretchedly tiresome, all that chatter, so I said to her, "Shut that squawking, shriveled nosferatu's mouth you eroded, festering corpse—"

"You are positively demonic Willard! You have a mind like an act of sodomy and the voice of a demon!"

Astounded by this outburst, for reasons which I have yet to grasp, I went into a cyclone of frenetic cursing and stomping. "Let mine be the voice of a demon then! Demonic?! Oh my, yes, I'll be demonic, devilishly demonic, demonized beyond reckoning, you nefarious offal!"

"I've had it with you Willard! After today, I'll—"

"You are like those walking cadavers that can't stop consuming their own livid flesh—"

"*Shut up! Get dressed! What* is *wrong* with you?!"

I think she may have continued but again I tuned out the excruciating frequency of her voice. Instead I focused on the task of addressing the incinerated hair issue. Luckily I happened to have in my possession—in my private collection of trinkets (collector's items) left from the various stage productions of my plays—a wig which fit my hallowed head with an unexpected and gracious certitude, as if created solely to rest upon my crown. The drawback to this solution was only that the hair of the wig itself was a handsome blonde, while it is well known that I am now a startling silver, while in my youth I was a black so intense that it was only a shade lighter than Appolonia's heart. With that out of the way I was nearly complete and finished dressing in short order. My meager breakfast was thoroughly unenjoyable thanks to Appolonia's incessant whining and nagging about getting out to the car, surely it must be waiting for us, blah blah blah, why was I so lackadaisical, on it went. At length I finally told her to go out to the car because it had been waiting the whole time.

"Well why didn't you say so?!" she replied, storming out of the kitchen.

In her absence I laughed to myself and followed her out to the front drive. Appolonia swooped down on me with a million questions as soon as I opened the door. "Oh?" I said playfully. "You don't see them waiting for us? Perhaps, just perhaps, that is because they are not coming." Appolina joined us in the crisp morning air.

"But...but..." My poor wife was as lost as a babe in the woods after that transaction of words. "Willard, what do you mean? They pick up and drop off every Nobel laureate on the day of the ceremony!"

Adjusting my cufflinks I stated matter-of-factly, "I told them not to bother."

"You what?"

"I turned them down."

"You did what?!"

"I told them we had made other arrangements in advance."

"*Other* arrangements? At least you did that, even if you had to be rude about it."

"Ahem...that is...not entirely."

"What does *that* mean, Willard?"

"It means," I said, making a conscious decision not to restrain the viciousness in my voice, "it means that I made no other plans, there is no car, no transportation to be had!"

"What do you *mean?*" Appolonia asked, astounded. "You mean to say that you did not arrange to be taken to the ceremony in a Rolls Royce or a limousine?!"

"Actually...oh! It slipped my mind. I *did* arrange something altogether 'fancy' that I am sure you will appreciate: I arranged for us to be taken via horse and carriage. We've already got you, the thing I'm waiting for is the arrival of the carriage!"

"Oh! You!" Appolonia charged at me then but our daughter intervened, restraining her mother.

"Don't fret mother, I'll see what I can do about it. You just try not to let him get to you and stay presentable."

"Oh! I wouldn't listen to a word he says to me, but...well you hear the things he says!"

"I know, I know," Appolina said, regarding me with a poisoned glare. "He'll make a fool of himself today in front of the world, you can rest assured. We'll laugh at him then."

"*Why—*" I began, but Appolina rushed inside with such haste that I was unable to launch a suitably scathing retort. My only alternative was to attack her mother then but she was turned away from me, a bemused look upon her face, apparently lost in the thought of my stumbling before the very persons I sought intellectual mastery over. Of course, our own car had been stolen by that mongrel Nihls, curse him, because he considered his wages to be unsatisfactory.

What a world! The trail of epithets in my mind kept me so preoccupied that I did not notice Appolina's return.

"Very good news father: you are a certifiable fool. On this of all days you turned down the generosity of the Swedish Academy, when of course, if you had been following the news, the public Transportation Union and Taxi Drivers' Union are both going on strike."

This was certainly an unexpected, unacceptable revelation. "A strike? Of taxis...a taxi strike?! Public transportation strike?! How is this possible?!"

"Do you mean to ask," Appolina evenly said, "how could they possibly not serve your every beck and call, or how could you not be every bit as omniscient as you had thought yourself to be? It is a simple thing called forethought Dad. You're supposed to plan these things in advance." Augh! Her standing there, defiant flesh of my flesh, with her arms crossed, exuding such an awful self confidence....augh, I say again, augh! The memory is like a night with Appolonia, in and of itself.

So it was that we were indeed transported to the event by horse and carriage, a steep cost but the only feasible alternative as all our friends and associates were already waiting for us at the Stockholm Concert Hall. "I hate carriages," Appolina stated once we were inside the cursed thing. "Did you see the whip that man is using? It's inhuman, it is."

"That's all very well and good dear," I hissed, driven mad by paranoia, "but what on Earth is this...this *coachman* doing, stuck on the back of the carriage like that?!"

We looked in unison at the diminutive window behind my head—I was situated facing forward while the two women sat before me, facing the rear—to spy the young man wearing an overcoat and top hat, smiling politely in at us.

"I believe, "Applonia said, "that it is customary for a man to ride standing on the rear of the buggy."

"Yes," I said, turning back to them, "but to what purpose?!"

"Perhaps...well, maybe it has to do with all those children and their skateboards riding around hanging onto the backs of vehicles."

"Appolonia, that is the most absurd theory I have ever heard. Did you see the look on his face? With all the bouncing of the carriage over the road, and him pressed up against the hard wood, well it is fairly obvious that he is staring in here at the two of you getting his jollies rubbing against this hellish contraption! How much more obvious can it be?! And in public no less. The humiliation!"

I expected them to be incensed at the notion but instead found that my daughter and wife both were smiling sweetly at the rear window, waving flirtatiously even. Turning again, throwing a cast-iron glare at that onerous man of dubious intent, I could't help but to feel a bit cynical about the notion that these carriage rides could be considered romantic in the least. "Appolonia, you would do well to remember that you are a married woman."

"What about me Daddy?" Appolina asked, her question like a dagger as she displayed the wedding band on her finger. "What am I supposed to do about this?!"

"Why don't you take two arsenic and call the undertaker in the morning."

"Honestly Willard!" my wife spat. "Can't you for *once* show your own child some *human decency?* It isn't *her* fault that we're in this mess. And how much is this extravagant waste of time costing us?! Answer me that Willard! What do you think we're made out of? Money?"

"If they are in the business of making money from dregs these days then yes, you and your daughter do qualify."

"Quite a stretch there, Pops," Appolina snickered. "Could it be that your limited mind can't support any other comebacks than name-calling? Have you even attempted to argue one point of reason in the last hour? Twenty-four hours? Twenty-four years?! Your enfeebled brain isn't up to the task, it would seem."

"I've said it before, and I'll say it again: I, dear lady, am a genius. They all agree! That is what constitutes this day."

"'A fool always finds a greater fool to admire him,' as Nicholas Boileau once said."

"Oh, how I do hate you!"

"'People hate the ones who make them feel their own inferiority.' Are you familiar with Lord Chesterfield?"

At this I first raged, bellowing, then immediately stopped, a sublime smile etching itself across my face. "Why yes dearest, I am quite familiar with Chesterfield. It was *he* who said, and I do agree, 'Women are to be talked to as below men, and above children.' En garde, little one!"

For a moment Appolina's face remained composed. What happened next though defied reason, defied me: the little wench began to laugh, furiously, despite my protests. Before I could mount a comeback worthy of the prized mind that rests within my cranium that bothersome fool of a coachman behind me let slip with a giggle, ever so slightly, earning him the wrath of Pretorious, the full unmeasured wrath of Pretorious! "Now you see here!" I shouted in English, intending to rap on the rear glass with that lovely, distinguished, sterling silver-tipped cane I so cherished. This is not what happened. No, instead, the metallic tip of my cane was thrust through the brittle glass with excessive force, sending hideous shards and fragments spraying into the man's eyes, nose, and mouth, and the handle itself visited devastating abuse on the hapless man's unprotected face.

The whole event rendered him, quite understandably, unable to maintain his loathsome grasp on the rear on the carriage. Off he went, flying onto the hood of the car behind us. Worse still, at the sudden crash of breaking glass and disfigured shrieks of anguish, the horses both bolted, in differing directions unfortunately...or perhaps I should say fortunately because instead of two horses dragging us with their fully disturbed strength one managed to break free, leaving us at the mercy of only one equine nut case. The driver worked with all the skill he had at his meager disposal but still we found ourselves careening off the roadside and plunging into a dank wilderness. The imbroglio of sensations and sounds that followed masked the details but I can say this: we found ourselves mired in a semi-frozen mud pit among a gnarled grove of trees, without a trace of either the driver or the one horse which had brought us that far.

No need for us to communicate existed. We were all alive, unfortunate as it may have been, and capable of leaving the carriage under our own power. For this very reason I leapt into the mud first and offered Appolonia and Appolina each my assistance in exiting the stranded carriage, only to have them hurl insults at me. This made all the more satisfying my laughter when they stumbled in the mud and ice on exit, nearly falling into the muck. Basilisk glares were their only response to my good humor and in this mood we made our way out of the mire, through the malignant underbrush and blighted trees, up the embankment to the road. An eternity of curses was on the tip of my tongue when, before I could speak, a car screeched to an unsteady halt mere feet from where we stood.

The window rolled down revealing a friend of mine, Reginald Ivar, a half English/half Swedish son of the infamous British expatriate Marla Combs, but that is a story I refuse to go into now. “Pretorious! My Lord! What happened to you man?!”

“Why, whatever do you mean?”

Appalled, he looked us over as he leapt from the idling vehicle, the overly polished sheen of which insulted me to no end. "Are you hurt? Are any of you in need of medical assistance? I can take you to the hospital, there is one close by..."

I tried to laugh the suggestion off to allay any fears he might have or inspire. "No, no, we've never been better although, I will admit, we were involved in a bit of an accident here. The fact remains that we are running late, confound it all! Circumstance has all but shackled us on this morning my friend. Would you be so kind as to escort my family and I to the Swedish Academy?"

The thought seemed to boil Reginald's brain in a cannibal's white-hot cauldron, my words stoking a fire which instantly assassinated his pleasantries. "Are you mad?! Looking like that! They'd have us shot before permitting you to enter the ceremonies in such a hellish state."

"Ha ha, Reginald, he's always such a jokester Appolonia." Only after I produced a sum of money sufficient to do more than cover his petrol expenses did Reginald's stance change. The simpleton just could not wait to hold the door open for us, as though he were a beggar to let that amount of money spin his attitude around so! It made me want to urinate on him directly, then and there, but my better judgment dictated that I should at least wait until after we arrived at our destination.

"Please, I insist Willie. You just make yourself comfortable." Willie! He had the audacity to call me by that abominable name, in the hopes of what?! Some fraudulent camaraderie?! The leper! So it happened that we were driven the remaining distance in Reginald's car, which reeked of evergreen and polished leather, nauseating me to the point that I had to roll down the window hoping the fresh air would prevent an embarrassing act of vomiting. As we neared our destination I queried him on the happenings of the day and the King's general mood. "No, no, I'm afraid he won't be there. He took his leave just before I left...something dastardly came up. Seems as though the *Danish scum* are at it again!"

"Oh," I said, shaking my head. "At least he wasn't held up on my account."

"On the contrary old chum, he was quite fed up with waiting as it was, but his advisors had convinced him to wait just five more minutes. That was just before he received word of the *Danish scum* and their troglodyte tricks."

"Curses..."

"But, I must say, good job on the prize-winning work Willie. You have my most sincere appreciation and congratulations on a victory that was, in all honesty, long overdue."

"Yes, yes, no need to carry on about it so, I'm not one to revel in his triumphs or gloat, or anything of that nature." Appolina burst into laughter on hearing this remark, so I cast my venom her way when Reginald was not looking.

"Come off it Willie, everyone who is even semiliterate knows that *A Serenade to Beauty Everlasting* was the most inspirational volume of poetry to be published in the last decade, easily. Perhaps in the last century, although others may debate the point with me."

Mother and daughter alike emitted a deep sigh after he made that asinine statement, and to disallow either of them time to make a snide remark I chimed in with, "Ah, well, perhaps, yes maybe. It could be that I beat the pants off everyone else going all the way back to Shakespeare."

"Their pants and their knickers! Then hung the sorry lot of poetic pretenders and 'woe is me' whiners out to dry, that's what you did," the sniveling little sycophant gushed. Oh, how I wanted to brand his face with a red-hot iron!

Instead I came up with a far more devious plan. "Reginald,

you've met my daughter before."

"Appolina is it? Hello dear."

With a grimace she said, "Yeah, hi."

"I've often remarked to myself, *Reggie*," I continued, "what a lovely couple the two of you would make. You are unattached these days, are you not, *Reggie?*"

"Willard!" Appolonia began but, fortunately, we arrived before she could launch into a bloodsucking attack. Furthermore, before even I was aware of it, a horde of lackeys descended, helping us, helping us, oh good God, their despicable helping! Only after being "helped" from the car did I manage to free myself of their sinister hands and the probing, seeping orbs in their eye sockets. During the whole affair Appolonia tried unsuccessfully to whisper scolding unsavories to me while Reginald tried unsuccessfully to engage Appolina in conversation. Finally she showed him the ring on her finger and he shut his mouth after that.

Those hateful lackeys ushered us into the exquisite building before I even had the opportunity to marshal my thoughts, gain any bearings, take in the sight of the place where my destiny was to be fulfilled. At last I shall attain fellowship, I told myself, yes the fellowship I had so desperately dreamt of the proceeding night, an unbreakable fellowship of spirit and intellect with the others worthy of being awarded the prize, being nominated, even those merely in attendance. A fool of some sort rushed ahead of me as we entered a filled reception area adorned with the most lustrous decor. "Ladies and gentlemen, I present to you...*Willard Pretorious*." With a grand bow and sweep of his arm the fool stepped to the side and the fully astonished attentions of those present—the affluent elbow-to-elbow with those possessing a wealth of intellect—fell on me and the illusion of fellowship was shattered in my mind, cast aside to remain forever unsated, simply negated on sight.

The reason being? Their ghastly and profound pallor, as though the ghost of a dung heap just ran into the lobby, streaking, and demanded they all hand over their underwear.

Swayed by the compulsion to explain myself I stated, "I, ah, heh heh...that is, I had an...an accident." After that it was all a blur. Some person or another escorted me about by the elbow, gently, introducing me to the persons who were significant enough to be introduced to, whizzing me through the facility while I smiled at times that seemed to me appropriate and, when questioned about any matter, I reiterated the fact that I had been in a grave accident involving two horses, a whip, and a man with a mouthful of glass. This line of conversation does not seem to be quite apropos in hindsight.

One thing that I did quite clearly glean in my dazed, sleep-deprived state was that I had been actually awarded the Nobel Prize in literature earlier, *in absentia*, but since I had arrived (un)fashionably late I may still make the speech as the designated time for this had not yet passed. "Do you feel up to the task Mr. Pretorious?" they wanted to know. "Shall we call a doctor for you, Mr. Pretorious?" they asked. "How lucky you are to have had your family on hand, Mr. Pretorious," they said, rather idiotically.

The proclamation, "I'm up for it," slipped out before I could actually consider what it was that I was saying.

"Very good," they replied. One of them even confided, "A good thing too or they'd have your head..."

We passed by a group of neanderthals who seemed vaguely familiar to me. There they were, gathered like a clutch of fly pupae, grinning like the mindless marionettes they always have been: the trustees! The representatives of the unmentionable college that is witless enough to employ Appolonia: they did manage to locate the gathering after all. What a despicable bunch of nonentities, they'll ruin my day, I told myself, my memory of the day, any food I consume today, even the very air which I breath...all of it! Curse them, a thousand times curse them! I nodded politely to their envoy with a smile dripping of honey and vinegar. It came to me as I acknowledged them that I wouldn't have it any other way; this triumphant moment would crush their meaningless lives beneath its terrible magnitude.

The thought was so entertaining that it became something of a time warp as I was so focused on it I was unaware of reality. Before I could fathom what was transpiring someone jostled me, then shoved me forward, and I found myself standing before a podium amid a polite applause. Suddenly every cut and scratch and scrape screamed seething soliloquies; my blonde wig felt as though it had become a ten-ton Chinese instrument of torture; the burned scalp beneath the imbecillic wig throbbed as the mind under it tried to summon those words I had insisted on memorizing. They think me insignificant? Foolish? Well! I would prove them wrong! And so I began quizzically handling the microphone mounted on the podium, trying to discover the source of that dreadful ringing, buzzing, infernal squealing, I loudly asked, "Is this thing on? Is it giving me feedback?" Realizing that the piece of junk was indeed most embarrassingly on I launched into the typical "thank you" speech that one would expect to find in an oration following such an honor. This was not the substance of what I wanted to say though, no, however long and eloquent my beginning I wanted a personalized Pretorious moment to come to the fore, a message to be remembered for all time. The sweetened words and swirling thoughts were these:

"I'll always remember my boyhood idol, Prometheus, the Greek bearer of light who sacrificed himself so that humanity may know the wonders of intellect."—*look at them all now, they have to acknowledge my manifest superiority*—"From his noble sacrifice stems every achievement of man; from his torment came our ability to ease suffering."—*sons of dogs, ha ha*—"No, I have never taken his example literally, but I do believe that one should devote his life to striving for perfection in the world around him."—*yes, you have to just sit there and take it don't you*—"To devote one's life to shedding light on the beauty that humanity can achieve, this is the vocation I have humbly sought after my whole life long, and if I have even been just partially successful then I am eternally thankful to the grace of the Almighty for empowering me to do so."—*I'll thrash them with a mace, yes, I'll smash every so-called intellectual you put before me*—"What the world of literature is faced with now, though, is not attaining the illumination of culture, of education, of everything which defines civilization."—*not only that, I'll take your wives to boot*—"The problem we face is a troubling darkness."—*I'll impregnate them, hmm, yes, it is only right for the most glorious to spread his seed around*—"This is not a darkness on the horizon, nor is it a darkness that we, as humans, naturally carry within us."—*and if you have a problem with that why, I'll have to kick your teeth in, you neanderthals*—"The problem facing the sanctified discipline of literature is one of certain individuals, certain persons passing themselves off as authors, who have an alarming propensity for inflicting their personal woes on others with no intention of addressing the human condition in terms of providing solutions."—*and if your females have a problem with that I'll deal severely with them as well*—"It is to these reprehensible, irresponsible, immoral sorts that we must turn our attentions."—*yes, I can see it in your eyes now, you all have to bow to me whether you like it or not, ha ha*—"You see, it is my firm conviction that art is meant to uplift."—*but my wife, curse her, where is she, she's not here, no, no, that cannot be*—"By examining only the base trifling of rakish anti-heroes we find nothing to uplift the masses, and furthermore by looking at something wholly evil simply for the sake of looking at it—and nothing more—we bring not enlightenment but its antithesis."—*you bitch, how I do hate you*—"We must, as the curators of the world's cultures, be stringent in our tolerance of those who seek only to inflict harm on the mind by exposing it to cruelty after cruelty after cruelty with no other intent than to cloud it with injustice."—*I'll slice your rancid flesh, slit your goiter of a throat you harlot*—"There is much to celebrate in the miracle of diversity that is man; let us instead focus on that."—*her infirm breasts and horrid garble of a voice, not that I miss any of it, but with no evidence of that blood-sucking tick I'll have to assume she has decided to humiliate me on my day of days*—"The beauty of everyday hopes and aspirations eclipse even the most dreadful calamities in that they can make the common man an emotional and spiritual giant, and in that no event, no matter how cataclysmic, can extinguish these so-called 'everyday' dreams."—*her and that whore's bastard I've suffered the indignity of calling daughter, both of them, I'll strangle them when we get home*—"This is the true essence of *A Serenade to Beauty Everlasting*, the universal truism that yes man is capable of rising above circumstance, indeed, that he will always prevail, you pus-filled skin sacks and your insufferable sucking, sucking, always bloodsucking, the torture that I know as your existence is as pleasant a thought as a date with a barbed-wire speculum and an elixir of horse snot!"

Oh dear, thought I.

In my frenzied, fogged, feverish state my self control and subconscious strife managed to exchange duties, if only for a moment, and the result was a hall full of luminaries—vibrant minds—hushed, ashen, outrage fortified in every one of them, and in their horror they were doubly horrible to my mind...*as Appolina had prophesied!* In the split second that I diverted my eyes to her grinning baboon's head in the crowd—yes, she had indeed been present all along—my muse created a thousand and one new combinations of letters, each a curse, each more dreadful than the one which preceded it. Then, in the next split second, I thought to myself: *Ah! Yes, I will use "the accident" as an excuse.* How very delightfully convenient! Perhaps I should always arrive late, claiming to have been injured in an accident, deliriously dripping verbal demons from the psychic wounds incurred by head injuries. How very perfect it would be! But no, no, instead of taking that path, facing the soundless chasm that had once been an appreciative audience, I blurted:

"Oh?! Does it shock you? Does it indeed? Ask yourself, honestly and truly, is this such polite company that your ears sting after such an outburst? Well!" I hesitated, watching Appolina mouth to her mother, *He's lost it!*, but this only spurred my confidence on. "Ha ha! Well, it is okay, yes, this is good, it is all right, I can accept this. But what I cannot accept are the filth peddlers whom fashionable critics embrace as the scions of worth in the world of literature! Yes, those very words I spoke moments ago, if you can believe it dear friends, were from an award-winning, best-selling book of similar tone and overall message throughout its intolerable duration, yes, a novel and novelist whose names I shall not deign to mention, but one whom you would all be quite familiar with. Yes! The very words and sentiment which only moments ago murdered—in the most bloody, mind-curdling manner—what had been a warm, exuberant atmosphere of humanity celebrating its crowning achievements: the most compassionate in arts and sciences, which is to say, enlightenment itself! If such a gathering for such a cause can be dampened by that one mere holocaust of a sentence, then I bid you, each and every one of you, to consider the impact of a whole volume of such dreary diatribes. This unspeakable person, at this very moment, is engaged in a highly publicized book tour, reading his soul-poisoning material to the youth at collegiate towns all across North America. It is unconscionable. We must take a stand now, or sit down forever!"

And, to a person, they all—*all*—rose to their feet in what can only be called uproarious applause! It should be noted that when I say to a person I discount those in my family as they are subhuman at best. Ha ha! What an inane bunch of drivel! Yes! And they bought it all up, much to Appolina's eternal disgust...I laid the tripe out and all these so-called "highbrows" dove right in like ravenous wolves trapped in a Siberian winter. Why not? Why not let that lousy hack Pollock take the fall, as it was quite clear that I had implied my dangerous words had sprung from a volume of his works—only later did I learn what actually *happened* to him during his book tour! Can words so easily sway minds back and forth like sickly reeds caught in a typhoon? Why, I testify in the positive, for the reason that when the mind is willing to believe...well, it simply believes! With that very thought on the tip of my tongue I smiled all the broader, the tight, thin scabs of Appolonia's scratches crinkling painfully in the process.

"I thank you friends, one and all, and in summary I would like to pass along a thought." Still those in attendance were standing, the applause dying down while the insidious duo slinked out the back door like the defeated curs they were. "The thought is this: beauty will always prevail. To all the perennial pessimists, I say flee from the rapturous light of reason, optimistic reason. To all the degenerate detractors, I say stand back and watch us, the healthy society, build while you in your frustration can only destroy." My word, I never had any inkling that it would be so frightfully easy. "The new millennium has begun, and from the ashes of doomsday millennium fears I see a brave, enlightened international community constructing a world we can all be proud of! Because as long as we harbor the *spark* of life, as long as the gentle rays of *reason* illuminate our path through the darkness, smiting ignorance, there is always hope." Ha ha! With those last words I bowed, concealing the searing pain caused by the action. Truly, I was at the end of my rope, so I was lucky to have finished when I did.

By the end of the speech my voice had grown so scratchy and weak that my words were barely audible, but there could be no doubt that my oration had overwhelmed paramours of intellect and dunces alike! The thunderous applause that I received was just enough to keep me from collapsing right there, slumping over on the podium like some cadaver ripe for the flies to feast upon. Yes, it was undoubtedly a glorious and lovely day, my perfect moment of beauty frozen forever in the museum of my memory, one that I shall look upon fondly until the end of my days.

The Ankle-Biter's Guide to Slithering

THE SPEECH

THE PROBLEM WITH DISILLUSION is it's something you invited to the dinner table, and it has treated itself to a quiet smorgasbord while you've distracted yourself with maps of hope, only to snap out of it and find the thing has eaten away your legs. There's no way in hell those maps are going to help you if you can't even move, so you might as well burn them in the vain attempt to keep yourself warm—staying warm is one of the most important aspects of treating shock—so reconcile yourself now to the fact that you have no hope left, and with no hope there is no future. Suddenly that wee little ankle-biter you thought you had under your heel is now a mower in the field of dreams and all the world is snoring because they just couldn't be bothered to give a damn one way or the other.

Why should they? After all, you're the one crawling away from the feast of life on your belly, not them. But that's not the main problem, which is is this: what is to be done in this new state of being, this disillusionment? How does one get by?

How about we look at what is conveyed by using the word itself. According to the *Webster Encyclopedic Dictionary of the English Language* released in 1967—somewhat out of date, but so the notions we have to discuss—*disillusionize* means "to free from illusion, to disenchant" so let's chew on that for a bit. Hmm, the flavor of enchantment, or more precisely enchantment gone sour. Enchantments ...dreams...illusions. Here's the key to the whole thing, this illusion business. To suffer disillusion one must first suffer illusion, yes? Phantasms of the mind telling us whatever we want to hear. Mostly we think of ourselves as beset by dreams only during the night hours, that we only see illusions while we slumber, and discount those hopes throbbing in our hearts during all our waking hours. Oh, those maps we had...oh well...at least we still have the pleasure of unconsciousness, yes? That poses an interesting problem. When one is disillusioned what dreams may come? What dreams may come indeed. Perhaps a box of chocolates that melts before you get to enjoy it, perhaps the sound of music delighting your ears and distracting your mind, maybe a pretty woman or your best friend's wedding, or some of your other favorite things. Perhaps, yes, perhaps. But with disillusionment changes take place not only in you, am I wrong? Does the world itself change? Or is it just the way in which we see the world?

Enough about this disillusion nonsense I say. What is there in life to be disillusioned about? Life, as they say, is beautiful. I suppose then that leaves only death and the underworld for those of us who are to be considered ugly. When the cheerful acceptance of maxims which stress happiness, triumph, and bliss is a thing to be striven for in polite society—which is to say beautiful society—such acceptance can be called beautiful then. As a society we wouldn't be yearning for something *not* entirely beautiful would we? No, no...no! We must remind ourselves that life is beautiful, bestowing its beauty on any and everything imbued with its miraculous spark, and so being alive...why that makes us beautiful too! Whether this is a beauty which is everlasting is neither here nor there. Being alive, being beautifully alive, we must then dutifully condemn those in our ranks who insist on viewing only the darkness as reality, or insist on seeing it at all; yes they should all be condemned! Kind sirs? Are you applauding me here? Oh, well, I don't know what to say. Where are my manners...thank you, thank you one and all for the strong embraces, but let us use caution at this juncture. Perhaps we don't see eye to eye just yet. Let me find a ladder or at least a soapbox to stand on.

As I understand it the playing field lies thusly: life is beautiful, therefore if we qualify as being alive we are beautiful, so then society at large is beautiful, which in turn means that those dissenters and detractors of society are as revolting as a seeping leper's scab, by which logic we must place those ugly sorts—let's call them *undesirables*—in the unliving category because, after all, life is reserved for those who are ravenously beautiful! Have I lost anyone here? Well, let's see then. The undesirables cannot possibly be left among us, no, they should be put with the rest of their unliving brethren. Underground with them then! Sure, why not? We'll bury them under an avalanche of our beautiful dirt and they can rest underground, as tradition demands of the dead.

But enough of this dwelling underground, it feels as though we've been impaled on the subject a good forty years or more. Let's examine conditions above ground, shall we? What are the basic elements of the lovely life? Frivolous cruelties, antagonistic delights, tiny trophies, and monumental woes. These components make up a cycle of ridiculousness that nobody wants to break free of. "Whoa now," you're saying to me. "What's this! Only a minute ago you were extolling the virtues of the beautiful life! Here here," all the kind sirs of the world are saying in unison (at least those listening to me).

Let me explain that. Yes, if blithe acceptance of platitudes can be beautiful then one thing leads to another and so on and so forth and the end result is that the brush of beauty paints everything, without streaks no less. Where can the frivolous cruelties be found? How about those pesky antagonistic delights, where is the evidence? In the constant criticism of your spouse's dinner, in cutting off your fellow travelers and giving them the finger, in prank calls at three in the morning, in laughing at that obese elderly neighbor who can hardly leave the house, in making up the lies that get our siblings in trouble or later our schoolmates suspended or later our coworkers fired, in making up some great past lover just to wound your mate's pride, in beating those who don't look like you with your fists or any other available object, in spitting on a person from the elevation of a bridge or balcony, in laughing in the face of some "loser" who just asked you out, in anonymous notes left on windshields, in not telling a lover about that little thing called gonorrhea carried inside you, in kicking the dog, etc. Frivolous is defined as being silly, trifling, of little weight, worth, or importance, so I think the above examples do qualify as they are all committed for reasons of little weight, and certainly they are cruelties, antagonistic in nature, and if we do not get a delight out of laughing at cripples and cutting off other drivers, well, I implore you kind sirs, tell me what then is the definition of a delight?

Yes, now you are scratching your chin and saying something like, "Okay, you've illustrated some points, but isn't it true that after our siblings get their behinds beaten red for our lies we buy them a lollipop? Or, if we can't buy it maybe we'll steal it, but that's beside the point. You see, dear jaded fellow, not only do we get those we love in trouble but we take care of them in their sufferings. The sugar provided by a lollipop soothes the soreness a throat experiences after wailing and crying. Ho ho! Now how about that? And just maybe that other driver needs to be 'taught a lesson' so that deaths and injuries resulting from poor driving can be avoided. No sir," you are most likely saying, "that is not a delight is it, preventing unnecessary deaths and wasted vehicles. That is a civic duty! Still you haven't 'enlightened' us—so to speak—on the subject of the tiny trophies and monumental woes."

Haven't I? Oh, well then, let's see. The greatest cause for communal celebration, our national pride, should serve as a decent example of what our society is like. Ah, the great land that gave birth to us, what's there not to celebrate? National pride is a good thing indeed, and being such a good thing it wouldn't hurt to take a look at the greatest application of national pride. It involves sending our youngsters off to get their arms and legs blown off in foreign lands so that chemical companies, medical suppliers, metal works, vehicle corporations, airplane manufacturers, computer developers, and, of course, our governing body, can put some money in their pockets. When our youngsters come back sans body parts or minds we can fashion a piece of metal like a fancy belt buckle, only a lot smaller than a fancy belt buckle, so they can wear it when they are feeling especially patriotic, if they are still so inclined. Sure, there are other tiny trophies to be had in life, but we're on the subject of national pride right now. Which brings us to the enormous and costly monuments we raise to commemorate the application of national pride—I mean, to commemorate the dead—which in turn is good for the tourism industry in our nation's capitol. You see, everyone comes away wealthy, or happy, after these events except of course those who made sacrifices for the cost of oil or to help our pals the French beat on some people whom they had invaded, only to have the French flee the scene after we showed up. At least we got to blow a lot of things up so the news anchors would have something to talk about between pitching the various trendsetting technologies and products. Goodness gracious! That does sound like a bunch of savagery, doesn't it, so maybe I'd better say "badness gracious."

"Well now," the kind sirs of the world are thinking (don't deny it), "You are a reprehensible lout to attack the sanctity of warfare in the United States of America. People, good people, gave their lives to make sure the Vietnamese were living under a democracy, even if that's not what half the country wanted. Furthermore, would you insult the policing action in the Balkans that prevented the atrocities in the Yugoslavian conflicts?!"

Ah: that's just it! When it comes to human rights—preventing suffering, ethnic extermination, systematic rape—well now that's time for a "policing action" as there's not enough to it for a lot of money, that is, there's not enough for a war in it. I mean, who's going to support ground action to stop genocide, of all things? Don't laugh, I'm being serious. Above all we pulled out the first time around allowing the atrocities to continue, so aren't we Milosevic's buddies after all?

"Oh! How can you?! What insolence!"

Please, kind sirs, let's not have the discussion degenerate into name calling and such. I merely point out that the Serbian thing was no war, merely a policing action, and as such not a cause for national pride (as pride only comes from doing the right thing, right?), therefore it was not a war and should never receive the benefit of a monument—

"Here, here! I take issue with that statement, you faceless author! Come out from behind these pages and let's settle this."

You *would* say that. However, I would say that it was a policing action.

"It was not!" would most likely be your reply.

To which I would say, You said so yourself.

"Why, I did no such thing! You put words in my mouth you nincompoop, because I'm not actually involved in this conversation. I am just a literary device! Now are you ignorant, or what?"

Well, let's just keep the discussion moving, eh? Where were we anyway, all your squabbling is breaking my concentration. Ah yes, the heaven-sent beauty that we are all enamored of: trifles, agony, and the delights of trophies and woe. What is the cause? Egocentric view, which is in turn the result of our limited interpretation of our physical senses. With all the sounds, sights, and sensations in creation aimed directly at me, standing directly in the center of this beautiful sensory maelstrom, how can I not be so damn important? I am, after all, right at the center of it—from where I sit at least. If I am the center of it all, if I am that important to have all of existence gravitating around me, then doesn't it fit to think of everyone else as not all that important by comparison? When we have our minds infiltrated by this line of "thought" there is nothing but a terrible butting of heads day and night worldwide and all the that our senses are trying to tell us, the root of all this, is cast aside in the resulting tumult.

It is simple enough, kind sirs, to figure out how to act correctly with the information our senses provide us, but damn what a pleasure it is to behave poorly! The slumming of our morality is so chronic, so debilitating, and we've such an aptitude for it! Oh my, I'm getting worked up again. Maybe it's just me. Maybe it's the proliferation of easy-outs we provide ourselves, as a society. Maybe it's too easy to reciprocate hate, to leap at the chance to *feel* justified and righteous. Guess that means we suffer, as individuals, from a low supply of righteousness and justification in our lives...and in the way in which we choose to live, eh? Why else would we be starved for the opportunity to be justified? It couldn't be that we simply like to manipulate situations so that we are continually wronged in order to get attention when our angry voices ring out. Yes, truly, it can make you feel as though you are the king of the world when the spotlight shines on your indignation.

But all this, these late-night delusional musings, it's all just circular reasoning every bit as self-serving as what I accuse others of. So go ahead and dismiss this. I'm giving us all one more easy-out. What, do I have to put sugar on top? Let's talk about something else, you and I, together, we'll talk about something else and have a great laugh. How about the wonders abounding in nature?

Nature. Hmm. Now there's a topic for discussion. We should know a great deal about it, being, you know, a part of nature and all that, along with being immersed in it day and night. Yes, the wonders of nature! You know it well, do you? Good, good, that'll make things so much easier. Here is the true beauty, I think, here in nature. Just look at the rich blue sky looming overhead, so vast, so glorious, that it almost makes the knees quiver to attempt comprehending it. With the boundless jewel that is our sky enveloping us day and night we can look forward to the striking hues of the sunrise and sunset. Obviously, knowing about nature as you do, I won't go into the specifics of just why the sky is blue, in fact you probably know better than I! So when I say that the condensation of our breath on a ball bearing is representative of that same atmosphere, in the scope of the galaxy—or worse still the universe—why, I'm sure you're already quite aware of that puny, fragile condition. Imagine that, a tiny little ball bearing resting on your fingertip representing our boundless planet drifting through space, the condensation of hot breath representing our enormous sky. Sure, and how about those beautiful sunsets and sunrises anyway? Why should I even bring the subject up, I mean you are the educated ones after all. It would be worthless of me, even worse it would be utterly contemptible, to mention the volcanic eruptions it takes to give us the most lovely sunsets, so full of startling colors. Those particles of ash that would be so distasteful to discuss, carried in that flimsy and rather insignificant atmosphere we just talked about, give the diminishing light something to reflect off of, livening up those sunsets with a wider spectrum of colors for all to enjoy. Are those ash particles the remains of children blown to smithereens in the eruption? Maybe they're the thousands of acres of precious jungle and endangered species evaporated in the event.

I know, I know. Even if we are not in control of ourselves, even if we are prone to the casual idiocies of our fellows, surely we have at least managed to coexist with the wonder that is nature, or better yet managed to master it through the discipline of science. True, only about nine hundred million people met their ends suffering from the major viruses and bacteria in the last hundred years, a pittance really. Let's not go into those who were pummeled by tornados and tsunamis, cooked to death by wildfires and volcanoes, swallowed up by the ground or those cuddly big cats. Even if we could achieve this "mastery" wouldn't it just be the mastery of a ball bearing or, more specifically, the space between the ball bearing and the condensation of your breath? My, that would be a triumph!

"*But what about the triumph of human virtue?!*"

Ah, well, thank you for bringing it up, I was just about to get to that! You see, it is my contention that the overwhelming misery of existing in this world *is* the very triumph of humanity's true "virtues." Through avarice—unending avarice—and our petty and spiteful carryings on we have ensured that we will all be vastly unfulfilled at best. So what is left for us? We can give up.

"What?! That's insanity! It's insanity and I'll have none of it."

Oh yes, it is easy, if I am insane, truly insane, it should be so very easy. Ignore me! You should, honestly. Say to yourself now, with a clear, unadulterated conscience: I am sane and I don't have to listen to this. I am sane, my sanity is intact, I am most pleasurably sane, thank you very much, and I for one will remain quite comfortably unmoved by the ranting of a madman, a lunatic, because everything you've expounded upon has been nonsense and rubbish. Go on ahead; say it. Well now, I can't hear you so I guess I'll have to keep going. Oh, on a side note, if I really am insane then what are you worried about? Your sanity should keep you afloat in the flood plain of my thoughts while my torrential verbiage thrashes itself into no more than a watery, innocuous mess. Why in the world should stable, healthy persons have need to fear words scribbled on a paper in some far away place, who-knows-where, by a person they don't and never will know? As for those who are emotionally unbalanced, well now, the damage is already done to them isn't it? I've got no control over that, or how they may point to my words as an excuse for their poor behavior (behavior that is exhibited in others who haven't read me even! How about that, eh? Were murders committed before *Natural Born Killers* came out, or *Taxi Driver?* Hmm, well that has nothing to do with my writing so let's move on...). Now I sense you have little option than to read on anyway, don't you, as a healthy and pleasurably sane mind should withstand any amount of rubbish it is confronted with, isn't that correct kind sirs? Hmm...

Yes, right, so I was talking about giving up. Yes you! You and I both, all of us, need to give up and accept things as they are. Give up your box of chocolates and your favorite things—you can't hold onto them anyway now, as they've been stripped from your grasp by the beautiful society—and find it in yourself to give up any latent resistance. When we learn to assimilate the contentiousness of nature and of our fellow man into our world view we will get along much better as we will no longer be surprised daily by the spit dropping onto our heads, by the neighbors laughing at us, by the person flipping us off after cutting in front of us. What a happy day that will be, when the mucus-filled spit slaps against your scalp from above and you are capable of chuckling to yourself, saying, "Yeah, gee, I remember how much fun I had as a kid doing that!" What a happy day indeed. When your brother is shot down in the next policing action, or your mother is killed off by those cigarettes, you'll slap your knee and say, "Yep! That's life," and then change the channel.

Oh, but what a trite bunch of hooey this is. Perhaps you'd like me to write about some heavy subject matter...no, no, I think it's best if we keep this simple and lighthearted. I refuse to go off on a tangent about corporate corruption and the cigarette industry highlighted in the example above. Why, it is true, tobacco is happily a thing of nature, it is natural, beautiful nature, and so is tar, yes that is true, in fact smoke itself is a part of nature, so why go into a rant about that! But then again uranium is also found in nature, but I don't see everyone rushing to suck on that stuff, so what gives? I think we've uncovered a double standard here, you and I, but let's not go into a rant about double standards...oh? You want to hear a rant about doubled-standards and the two-faced life? No, really, I'm just pulling your leg now.

Oh drat...that's right, you've no leg left to pull! I forgot already. That dreadful disillusion business comes back to haunt the conversation once again as it is the culprit of your legless condition. Hopefully you've gotten over the shock part, with the assistance of your burning hopes of course. You will find that with your disfigurement comes the label "undesirable" my friends, and bearing that label you will discover a great liberation. From your new legless position, like some tormented Weeble-Wobble or possibly still on your belly like a serpent, you can become empowered. Yes, empowered! From your new societal position, buried underground, you can become empowered! It's entirely too simple really. With all those beautiful giants lumbering above, an insignificant undesirable such as yourself is in the perfect position to bring them tumbling down. Now *you* can play at being the ankle-biter. What other position are you in than to chew on all those lovely well-heeled ankles?

No, no, let's not think of this as something done out of sheer spite. Consider it an act which attempts to affect some form of societal change. Sure, that's it. Just keep your eyes trained on the beautiful ankles of society, keep sharpening your teeth, and you can't go wrong. Perhaps your bite may even spread this intellectual infection to others? No, I'll refrain from launching into a tirade about the sanctity of gutter sickness at this point, really, I will. The important thing is to spread your new world view around among the populace at large, to replicate the thought that perhaps not all is well, perhaps we should be looking at the problem from the underside as those who are afflicted see it...not looking down on society's woes from the lofty position afforded the middle and upper classes by their affluent status. After all, it is the underside of a beast that is most vulnerable to attack, is it not? So let's everybody lose those legs, one and all, nationwide, for the good of your fellow man.

As an ankle-biter you learn not to worry about dentition. Let others concern themselves with that one. All you can do is concentrate on the act of biting and the time spent preparing yourself between bites. Here I am biting you from a typewriter (aha...even I succumb to ceaseless desires to keep romantic pretenses alive; I, like every other writer these days, use a computer!) with teeth made of ink carried by paper jaws, poisoning you with venom as weightless and fleeting as a thought. Despite being a world apart the distance from my mouth to your mind isn't so far after all, eh? Perhaps you'd like to try it sometime.

These are all just words though, curse them! Yes, curse them, that's what I say, curse them for being incorporeal, mere ink spots carried by paper or vibrations carried by the air. But then what manifestos and sayings, what rules and laws, are not just mere words, their value and strength existing only in our heads? It might just be that as an ankle-biter, as a detestable invalid cordoned off to live thankfully out of view of the beautiful people, you are not only out of their sight, out of society's sight, but out of their hearing as well. It might just be that their words are no longer capable of reaching you. Yes? Oh, yes, I do think so. So if their platitudes and regulations no longer hold any meaning, no longer form a thought structure for you to languish in, what is there to stop you from doing anything—absolutely anything—that catches your fancy? Hear me out kind sirs! Yes, it is true, this is my firm and resolute belief: that desperate disillusion, the obliteration of hopes and dreams, is the true liberator of mankind! Furthermore, it is affliction and disablement that frees us to move at will, to truly pursue our heart's desires. Soon enough the thought of those teeth sinking into your legs will be your most treasured memory, you can trust me on this.

The joy you experience may be compared to that of a private flogging to the public head. But let's not dwell on that comparison, for the sake of preventing headaches let us just move on, please. After all that we have shared in our discussion maybe it is best to stay here and progress no further. Yes, I think it best to relax after such an exhausting journey. Now that we have climbed to the summit of this Mt. Saint Helens of rubbish together, let us enjoy the view of the sunset and remember that life, as they are so very fond of saying, is beautiful!

FEELING DIRTY

"Wha' da *hell* that honkey been talkin'?"

"Beats mah ass blackinblue..."

"Sho' 'nuff, ain't got much beatin' tuh do, your ass bein' black as uh snake's belly at midnight!"

"Haw-haw Charlie man, he done tore you up like he Dracula an' shit, haw-haw!"

"Your mama ain't had no probem wit' me bein' dis black las' night, bitch."

"Oh jeah, bitch? Now how da hell she goin' do anythin' wit yo ass at night when she ain't got her no cat eyes? Hol' up, I'm needin' a flashlight jus' tuh see yo ass for conversin'."

"Haw-haw! Damn Charlie."

"The darker it be, the stronger it be, jus' like coffee."

"Haw-haw!"

"Damn young, dint know you was a poet an' shit, Mistuh Pretorious Blackass."

"Haw-haw!"

"Mah ass gots tuh be dis black bitch tuh make up fo' your ole-yeller self."

"Da-aa-ay-yay-am! You goin' sit there an' take dat shit Trey?"

"Wha' else he goin' do 'sides sit 'round and take it like a *toilet* jont. Callin' mah ass black, shee, he jus' sorry he so yellow dat he cain't go out at night, 'cause he turn midnight to high noon. Dat's why he goin' jus sit dere an *take* dat shit."

"Haw-haw!"

"Aw right Charlie, it's all good, ah feel fo' yo ass, honest now, straight up, I know it was tough an' all growin' up wit' your mama thinkin' you was your brotha's shadow and shit."

"Aw right 2000 Flushes. You jus' sit your ass there, I had me some burritos fo' lunch now, you jus' keep dat big mouth open."

"Haw-haw..."

"Bitch."

"Bitch."

"*Bitch.*"

"*Bitch.*"

"Haw-haw, come on now, don't let me be seein' da brotha-man goin' afta da brotha-man. Go on up afta wha' dat devil-man got fo' hisself. Shee-it now, you youngin's be amusin' a nigga an' all but calm dis shit down, on da reals now."

For a moment the three are silent, leaning against their broom handles, watching the crowd of creamy middle class with new clothes and backpacks and briefcases and glasses and styled hair and cell phones and soft hands all milling about, focused on some guy supposed to be an author who just seems to be ranting like a madman.

"Wha's all dat shit anyhow? Sound like mental chitterlin's an' Rockey Mountain oystahs served up cold."

"I be thinkin' he talkin' cannibal-like, dig?"

"Shee yeah, bitin' on people's leg and all. Whycome these folks listenin' tuh dat yang-yang an' not whippin' on his ass? Shee. Ain't no Hannibal-cannibal goin' roll up in my 'hood like dat, shee, not wittout gettin' hisself somma dis black man's foot up his hineside."

"Haw-haw! You know it, bro."

"Ain't nuttin' tuh be bitin' on dat skinny scarecrow leg besides."

"I done showed your *mama* how much meat I got on da bone *las' night*, dig?"

"Haw-haw, damn if he ain't tore your ass up like a cannibal-ass sumbitch. Dang-on young, you boys bein' a buncha haitas up in here..."

"All's I know is dis: I be up dere, or some bro, talkin' like dat? Uh-uh, no-how no-way. Da man be up in your grill in no time an' put a cap in your ass."

"Um-hmm."

"Sho' 'nuff, for real.

"Um-hmm."

"Damn straight."

"Ain't no lie..."

Only now is Charlie aware of the fact the his nephew has been standing within listening distance as he and his buds shot the breeze dead with their foul mouths. There's no need for a seven-year-old to be hearing that kind of talk, at least not as far as he's concerned. Feeling a little guilty he removes a five from his pocket and places it in the boy's hand.

"Go get somethin' tuh eat boy..."

Sure, it would be better without the kid around. Sure, the blood doesn't come up easily but with enough elbow grease he can do it. Always pushing the stinking mop around...it's a burdon, leaving its splinters in his hands, it's the truth. One day, though, one day he'll finally get rid of the blood.

"Yo yo yo...command central callin' Charlie...come on now son, wha's up? Blood?"

"On da reals now. What up wit dat blood foolishness? You been listenin' to dat sorry buncha hutchcome too hard my man."

"Didn't say nothin' 'bout no blood."

The blood is everywhere. People are slipping on it, choking on it, even letting it into their bodies. Not on Charlie's watch. He won't have any of it.

ALTITUDE

Motherfucking niggers, I swear, they'll be the death of me. Here we are in the middle of a pack-jammed author reading and not only are they lounging around, not working, they're scaring the fucking customers with their gutter talk! Why, I ought to...it was only a few days ago, last week maybe, that I heard them going on about Bill Clinton right here in the store, *on the floor no less*, during store hours, with all their "Bill ain't trippin', Bill ain't trippin', Bill da man" garbage. I should have fired them right there on the spot. I knew it then and boy am I ever regretting it today. Thank God we've got a real president in office now. Whatever. I'm the man here, I'll show them that much.

Two complaints about them in as many minutes! What are they thinking?! I'll give them a piece of my mind, I will! Rushing all around the store, smiling politely and excusing myself as I shove past costumers, and I can't find Jacobs anywhere. What is going on here? Yes, those niggers'll be sorry, I'll settle their hash so to speak, just as soon as I find Jacobs, yes, they will discover that a severe tongue lashing—the *most* severe—is what you earn when you screw with me. Things just *can*not keep going on this way, I mean really. It's bad enough that this guy is reading off a bunch of sanctimonious left-wing nonsense to an impressionable young audience—let's face it, all young people are as malleable in their morals as clay before it enters the kiln—and I may not be able to do anything about that, in fact I'll be prospering from the books sales, but I will be God damned if I will put up with these three any longer.

There he is! "Jacobs, come over here." He manages to tear himself away from the backed-up help desk and makes his way to me not quite as quickly as I'd like. "You see those three back there? I want them gone by the end of the day. You replace them with spics that don't know any English, got it? I don't want the new ones to be able to bother the customers. For God's sake, we have the reputation of our National Community Sensitivity Awareness Store Of The Year award to defend!"

"Uh...right away sir." He speeds away with a look of concern, probably because he could be torn to shreds—I mean we are talking about *three* blacks here! What he should really be worried about is the bass in his voice when he talks to me. Why, I just have to wonder what happened to professionalism—to mother-raping *civility*—in the workplace, and more importantly what happened to knowing your rank in the workplace? It is next to impossible to find good help these days. What am I supposed to do? Accept this kind of attitude?

Okay, maybe I am just a little tense, maybe I've been sampling a little of my product, maybe I should just "cool out" as they say. No! I have a Masters in Business Management! What do they have backing them up?! Nothing but a bunch of bleeding-hearts trying to choke self-respecting white men with a smorgasbord of regulations and laws and utter crap. I should suffer this nonsense? Hell, I've written three manuals on customer relations. I'd be surprised if those three could even sign their owns names. I'll see them dealt with first, then maybe reign in Jacobs' ego a bit. Give him what we in the trade call an "ego adjustment"...there are some women here that I'd like to give an "id adjustment" to but I'll think about that later. Now is the time to deal out retribution and I think these undesirables will find the deck stacked against them. I'll not let our reputation slide into the gutter. God damned sons of bitches want to use that kind of fucking language in my store? I'll have none of that!

Why, just a few months ago we had a reading from the Nobel prizewinner. How can we maintain that caliber of author readings with a staff that scares away the customers? For the love of Pete, we've got to be sensitive to the community or else 1) our sales will plummet, 2) we'll lose our stroke, 3) we won't be nominated for any awards this year. No bonus for moi? I don't think so. I'm not letting these SOB's take money out of *my* pocket. It's robbery is what it is! Attempted robbery! I should be reporting this to the authorities, I should. Who knows what these three are capable of?

I'm watching from behind the observation window now, but can't see them out there. Where did those three go? Where's Jacobs? Did they do him in when I wasn't looking?! They did! They killed him and now they're on the prowl for me! No, no. That's crazy thinking there, no. Somebody would've seen the whole thing, somewhere, and would be screaming their heads off. If not a customer one of the other workers at least. Where are the other office workers? Oh, that's right, out on the floor for the special event to keep an eye out for shoplifters. I realize now just why it's so quiet in here.

Well, well, well. I'm alone in here behind a one-way window that the customers can't see through, so why don't I just go ahead and lock the door? All these young men and young women to look at; my hand is already entering my pants, and I'm getting that familiar feeling...Christ I love my job...

CONTROLLING THE VIBES

I think I'm in love. William Pollock...hmm...how would Mrs. William Pollock sound? No, no, that wouldn't do, none of that outmoded tyrannical thinking for me, I'll still be Aubrey Mills, or maybe Aubrey Mills-Pollock, or how about Aubrey Pollock? Oh well, there's plenty of time to think about that later I suppose. Right now all that matters is the moment. Looking around at everybody else crammed in here to listen, well, I honestly don't think they have a full appreciation for this moment at all. I mean, just check the confused looks on their faces.

That whole story was pretty weird, I guess you could sort of maybe call it surreal? Possibly? Well, I guess it was not a story so much as, well, an essay or something. Who cares when it sounds so sweet, every word a delicacy for the ear rolling off that tongue, born of that alluring mouth. It makes my heart flutter sometimes thinking that he was speaking to me and me alone, just as if we were under a beautifully depressed willow tree by a scenic creek, at the edge of a gorgeous green field that marches on forever and ever, the birds chirping and the flowing of the water not entirely obscured by Bill's romantic guitar playing, an acoustic guitar, one that he fingerpicks some classical ballad on while reciting a story to me, just to me...oh God he is just too perfect, and just so in love with me, I know. I could detect his coy glances, he couldn't hide them from me during the reading. I picked up his vibe that he wished it were just the two of us here, alone, or maybe at that enchanted brook, but I sent him back my feeling that it was okay, I would suffer these throngs and masses of people just to be near, just to let him sing out his devotion to me discreetly, secretly, by reading works that seem politically subversive on the surface. Oh no, I know the real meaning, the hidden subtext, the message he's really trying to get across to me—just like he has for years—me and me alone. What a naughty one it was too!

Oh Bill, Bill, Bill...my beloved Bill...it's okay, dearest blossom of my heart. I know that you are hearing me through your acute empathy, just as I hear you, so no more words are necessary. Let's just give each other some breathing room, some room to breath, just for a bit, okay? All right then. Good. Love you too. Yes, I got the whole "perspective" aspect; good work on that one lovey. But honestly now...okay, thanks. Toodles.

I think I see Cedric over there, that guy from my homecoming...no, no, what in the world was I thinking? He's just another employee here. Isn't that the help desk guy? Maybe that's why I recognized him; I've sure enough talked to him more than my fair share of times. The atmosphere here is so friendly and open. That has to be the thing that draws me back here time and time again. I would say hi but he looks like he's in a bad mood for some reason. Guess they have him running around doing special stuff for the event here today.

It's the stuff like this, the whole thing here today, that make life easy for me. Every time I'm getting stressed at school I can come and just sort of chill out here, read a little and learn something new, just forget the tension. And God, if it weren't for their cafe I would've gone just absolutely in*sane* this semester. Not only do they make the best mocha ever but the staff are always so courteous. Best of all they are always sensitive to the plight of college students. If only the rest of them back home had experienced the poverty, the culture shock, everything to do with being a student at such a liberal university, they would be able to look at the world with expanded eyes as I do.

What's that Cedric look-alike help desk guy up to? I don't see him...oh. Wait. He's talking, more like arguing, with three seedy-types over there, in the corner. Man, just look at that. I don't like the way it's shaping up over there; they could get violent any second from the looks of it. Guess it's time to cut my losses and clear out before I'm just another victim on the news. Better to try the rest of the mall.

At least there's a mirror here that I can use to check myself in before leaving. Geez, I can't believe my hair got like this. It isn't too hard to fix but I just wanted to be perfect for this one occasion, is that too much to ask? Nobody's looking so I can finally adjust this stupid bra; God I hate underwire. I'd like to see men try putting wire in their underwear to keep everything in place. No, that's still not comfy, maybe a little more to the left...hey, what was that? I could swear I heard some kind of groan coming from behind the mirror, almost like a...like a...*a ghost or something!* Five...four...three...two... one...okay, I'm calm again. The whole thing with those janitors is bugging me out so bad, I just *have* to get out of here and calm down. Maybe get a gelati or something, some kind of veggie wrap.

That's what it is. I haven't eaten all day, that has to be the problem. It could be that Bill's works just overwhelm me with all sorts of emotions; he tends to have that effect on people. Yeah, it's got to be his mind-altering perceptions about the human condition. I know it's got to be that. Yep, either that or those new meds Dan put me on. It's just so crowded in here. Could it be that Dan made a mistake or something, I mean, just like a slight miscalculation or something? Nah. Maybe those money-grubbing pharmaceutical companies lied to Dan about the side effects that this stuff may have, like, on people and stuff. Like in that Kurt Russell movie where his daughter burns people alive? And that David Cronenburg movie about the drug that makes people have psychic abilities and all that. Maybe that's why I can communicate with Bill!

"Bread!" some little black boy is shouting, scaring me half to death as he runs by, and thank the Lord I'm already clutching my purse close because I hear they start fairly young. "Let them eat!" he screams on the way out, ahead of me, and everybody is looking this way. "*Bread!*" With his high voice trailing away down toward the pharmacy, sub shop, and fitness center the scene dies and everyone's attention shifts back to my caustic cherub and his book.

Wait. That one black guy, with the mop, he's still looking this way like he's...pissed or something? Is it, is he...is he looking at me?! Yeah, yeah I think so! All the times I've been here I haven't seen their kind lingering around the mall. If only I had paid more attention! Who knows how many are lurking in this place. Oh good Christ...did I leave the car unlocked?! Damn, oh damn, I'm such a stupid, stupid girl, just like Dan said. The portable CD player is even on the seat! Well, shit, I might as well consider it gone already. The main thing is to leave the mall without them getting me. Maybe I can get one of the security guards to escort me to my car...yeah, yeah, I think so. That's what I'll do. They think they've got me where they want me, but they don't, I'll show them that brainpower is the key; that's right, I'll outsmart them.

Just wait until my therapist hears about this. Dan, I have to remember to think of him as Dan, I try so hard not to get upset when he goes off about the dynamics of our relationship. Hush, hush. Enough of that. See you around Bill, maybe at the next store? Isn't that like two days from now? All right, it's a date.

DISINTEGRATING

The reading finished just in time man...the acid is peaking I think...holy shit, I never saw that pattern there before, it's like some kind of freaky techno maze and shit like that but I don't even like techno and shit like that dude..."We'd like to thank you for reading that tantalizing selection from your collected works, which are available today, by the way, in the special 'Meet The Author' section over here to the side, for those who are interested. Now I believe we'll open up the floor to questions for the author."...aw shit now man, that's low, that's so like, yeah, low man I can't believe I forgot about the questions and the answers but I don't even know the answers, hell, just get me the fuck outta here..."—wouldn't you agree?"...damn, agree with what?! What the hell did she ask?! Huh..."Well, considering my stance on the entire publishing industry, the American ethos, the self-induced condition we find ourselves in, the dead weight of the past bearing on us and the destructive pressure of the future dragging us down like a malignant pregnancy, not to mention how I feel about language in general, well I guess I'm so cantankerous that you'd be hard-pressed to get me to agree to anything!"...yeah dude, all right, that got 'em all laughing and whatnot and I feel like I'm falling down or up and the feeling I need to piss is too much TOO MUCH I NEED TO PISS..."But wouldn't you say that your work has had more influence on the writers of today than that of Pretorious or Gridly?"...come on now you lemon, don't try to flatter me, I don't take kind words from citrus fruit, I eat citrus fruit..."I couldn't say one way or another, honestly? You know, I just do what I do, I say what I need to say. If others are into that or, well, if maybe they're not, I won't let it sway me one way or the other. Aren't there any limes here?"...at least that freaky girl who kept staring at me had the decency to leave...wasn't she at the last reading?...

goddammit...something keeps touching me on the neck only I can't see it...they must all think I'm shit, yes, they're all against me, the fuckers, I should've known it when they all turned yellow..."Here you go sir."...some sort of woman just handed me of all freakin' things a lime, oh God..."When you look at the world do you really see such savagery or are you just, like, making it up, making it feel so oppressive because you're such a good writer, that is, able to just make it feel that way because you can make it all up in your imagination?"...the fear, the fear..."Don't take lemons. The lemons won't compliment you, don't trust them."...biting into the lime now like it's an apple and damn if I don't taste a thing man but whoa, look at the way they're all looking at me. That time when I cannon-balled into the lake where my grandmother had that smelly cabin and the water was so freezing cold and I was only nine? And I got ninety-eight mosquito bites in one single day? Why am I remembering that now? Whoa...this podium just moved..."Did anybody else see that or was it just me?"...dude man..."Pardon me, all right, but I for one just want to say that whole piece of yours is truly in bad taste. I have a brother in a wheelchair so there's nothing funny or amusing about people not being able to use their legs."...huh?... "Well, that's not really what my story is about—" "I don't care man, I'm telling you, it doesn't matter what it's about because it's in poor taste. Handicapped people aren't something to laugh at."...I still can't taste this lime..."Listen, I'm using...in this story, or piece, or whatever, you'll find a liberal use of metaphor—" "So my brother's just some kind of metaphor to you?!" "I don't even know your brother—" "That's right, exactly, you should be showing some consideration for the people out there, but you didn't, did you. Can't think of anybody but yourself!"...damn lime...fuckin' hell lime...why is it wriggling like that..."I think we're moving into exactly the territory I was talking about, or discussing, in my writing, we're moving into that territory—in this conversation—about perspective, or lack thereof...the limes! I won't suffer your scurvy anymore! No!"...and people are laughing, really laughing so hard, and that freaks me out even more but the podium gets trashed and now they aren't laughing so much, not laughing at all, and I think I'm still saying something about scurvy gotta warn them patterns techno bullshit patterns it's lovely I wish why is she looking at me it's all just a marketing scheme man when Ian Curtis hung himself was he really standing on a block of ice is that shit true she's not real these scurvy sons of bitches want to market me won't control patterns it's all a scheme a marketing scheme won't you racist sons of bitches collect the change god damn upper-crust pseudo-liberal kids want to buy a piece of me won't let won't illuminated mannequins won't

STINGING

The guy thought he was so smart. Now look at him. Four or five good smacks with a baton and you're the same as anybody else. Four or five good smacks with a baton and the stuff we all have inside comes out. I'm not going to go into why his pants are down around his ankles. The way he's struggling we can't get his privates covered up so I guess we'll just have to drag him out like this.

"Oh my God," some guy says.

We've been on to this Hollings guy for a while: distributing coke to "collectors" through the special order books. Not a bad gig, not bad at all. I mean, that car and that house, I'd like to see a bookstore manager get them on just a salary.

"I've got rights...I've got rights, you sons of fucking whores..."

Howie has his hand on the cuffs, behind the perp's back, and does the old crank trick which causes our man to cry out. Nobody could see what Howie did so we're all good.

All of a sudden we hear some sort of crash like something breaking and some guy is screaming up in front of the crowd...isn't that the dude they had taking questions when we went in? Isn't he like some kind of writer or something? "Eh Howie, you see that?"

"Roger that. Probably angel dust. Want to make a move?"

"Why bother. I'm guessing he'll be dead in a minute anyway from the looks of it. We got the big fish right here."

"What's the big idea!" Great, some of his workers. "This is police brutality! You'll be hearing about this! We're going to file a report, every one of us!"

"Hey, lady. We told you what was going on and told you to stay out of it. So he got his head busted 'cause he tried to take us out. That's what happens. His pants? You don't even want to know what he was doing in there, watching out through that mirror. Yeah, that's right. He won't let us pull his pants up but you're welcome to try. What? You don't want to?" At least that shut her up. I can't stand these people.

All of a sudden the S-bomb drops and we're directly at ground zero. I hear people wrecking stuff but it's so crowded in here that I can't see a dang thing. Things are crashing left and right across the store and some other bunch of workers are running our way. The only thing I want is to get this guy down to the station so we can get started on the paperwork. Look at what's happening to this place. No Jesus, no peace. That sums up these filth peddlers. I've been cool on Christ longer than most, I'll say that much for myself.

"What's going on over there?" Howie asks the frantic clerks.

"It the anarchists!"

"The antichrist?! Where!" My gun's out but I don't know what kind of good it'll do against Satan's earthly manifestation and all that.

"No, no, it's the *anarchists!* They're practicing for the next IMF conference or something!"

"What? IMF?"

"Our travel section is under siege god *damn* it—"

"Hey now, you watch your mouth pal—"

"Just do your job already and get these jerks under control! Will you? They're going to destroy the whole store at this rate, and then who knows what'll be next!"

"Well, what..." I can see from here what's going on but for the love of Pete, what am I here? Mall security? Come on man, I mean really.

Howie hands the perp over to me and taps his radio. "I'll radio in some back up, folks. We're only two men here all right? You just try and clear customers out of the store. Don't try to physically intervene on anyone's bodily happenings, you leave that to us."

While he's wrapped up in that mess I see a bug-eyed janitor slipping into the office we just busted this fool in. He slops a rotten-looking mop out and goes at the blood we left on the floor. "Sir, this is a crime scene. This room is off-limits. Sir?" Looks like we're going to have to forcibly remove that joker. Well, maybe Howie can do it. The way this guy is mopping up the blood...it's kind of scary, even to me. What's next? You plan an operation like this for months and this is how it goes. Say, there's that little black kid I saw running out of here before we made our move. He's running right this way! "Hey, will somebody get this kid under control—"

Before anyone can do something to stop it the kid runs up and kicks our perp right in the gonads and yells, "Crumbs!" Howie grabs the kid and the little punk bites his hand, so Howie maces him, right here in the middle of what we in the trade call a "situation"...not the best place to be macing little Black boys.

Before I know it the crazy janitor is trying to cram the bloody mop down Howie's throat and while I'm radioing for assistance some dumb motherfucker crawls on the ground and bites my ankle! I can't help it if

I'm stomping the guy's head into the floor because really, that bite stings like all hell. "Don't move, don't you move, you're under arrest—"

"*You saw what just happened!*" some Black Muslim is shouting. "*They want to turn back the clock four hundred years! We can die fighting or live in chains! Zion above! Babylon below! Death to Dr. Yakob's fascist überclass!*"

I don't know what the hell he just said but it was the straw that burned the camel's ass. An all-out stampede of freaked-out students comes crashing our way and I've got my gun out now. "Don't come any closer! This is an official order! Don't move!" The problem is everyone's screaming and I don't think they heard me and all of a sudden I'm knocked on my side with at least four IMF antichrists biting my leg and from where I am I can see that writer getting trampled in the chaos and I just wish I had kissed Betty good-bye because I might not see her again. A bunch of them are holding Howie down and yep, that janitor really is cramming the bloody mop down his throat. One shot...two shots...okay, I hit somebody that time, the punk slumps over and now they're scattering like roaches when you turn on the lights. I clip the janitor in the leg. No, I don't want to kill him...no, he's coming down to the station with us. Whether he leaves the station alive or not is another question.

"Officer down...officer down...repeat, we have a man down..." Even the feminists have stopped stomping the half-naked perp. In all of this nobody's tried to get the mace out of that kid's eyes, so he's still screaming his damn head off. Jesus! Look at my leg! I can't feel a thing...

Maybe it's Racist...

"...BUT I THINK WE HERE in God's land are experiencing an onset of white-niggerism the likes of which has not been seen before."

After missing a beat Radley asks, "Come again?" He does this intentionally to distance himself in the eyes of viewers, but is casual enough to avoid alienating the senator.

"Mike, let me put it to ya another way. My mama told me like this: 'Ya mix the whites and the coloreds and ya end up ruining the whole batch.'" He's in the limelight now, that's what he's thinking, the senator. He won't back down on his convictions. Not with the eyes of his constituents on him. "People, our people, the American people—and when I go and say that, I mean God's people Mike—are getting concerned, there's growing concern among them, them all, because you see it's concerning about this, this white-niggerism. It's a threat worse than any communist scare. What we're bearin' witness to, so help me, is the loss of the individuality of the species—the races, that is—the culture of...what I'm sayin' here is that the white culture, the culture of our white Americans, is gettin' lost! Lost in the shuffle it is. Where's the White preservation society? Federal funding is going into savin' buildings, savin' trees, savin' this and that, buildin' museums for all sorts of ethnic types. Sure, go ahead, I do think this is a good idea. But what about us? We built this great land out of nothing, out of wilderness, and now we're gettin' swallowed up like some kind of mad dog swallowing its own tail. That's just what it is, madness it is."

An emblem with a bald eagle carrying the words "Hardline Nation" is between them, mounted on the wall behind the chairs and the little table holding flowers that conceal the microphones. Mike Radley has been the host of *Hardline Nation* since its inception five years ago. Being located right in the hub of national politics a local District of Columbia TV channel decided to boost their news ratings by adding this segment on a weekly basis.

With the knowledge that he has all the makings of killer sound bytes and vid clips in place Radley strings the senator along, fully aware that when they run Gibson's outrageousness he too will be featured across the nation. "So when you say this, Senator Gibson, you are not making a comment against minorities, is that what you are trying to say? That this is merely an—in your view—defensive stance?"

"That is correct."

"You don't feel that these words may be construed by some as being inappropriately strong?"

"No, no I would not. No sir. Strong problems demand strong words, and even stronger actions."

"Oh?" Radley says, the "news clip of the year" light flashing in his mind like a series of atomic detonations. "Strong actions? I see." A contemplative pause, although not long enough for Gibson to speak. "And when you say stronger actions, I assume you mean steps to preserve the Caucasian American 'way of life' as you put it, but what steps are we talking about here? What steps do you propose?"

"Well now Mike, I'll tell ya," Gibson says, somewhat more laid back in demeanor, having realized that perhaps he has gone a bit far. "I think that decision is best left to the American people. I simply propose that this issue needs to be looked at, to be examined in some official, or unofficial, capacity."

"How do you mean that Senator?"

"I meant it just the way I said it."

They've already entered their circling stances, ready to "play the game" for the rest of the program. That is to say nothing of any relevance will be revealed so, to be honest, I see no point in continuing to focus on them. But just who am I to be making these decisions anyway? I mean, who am I to you?

It may just be that I am beyond persona non grata. Yep, maybe I'm just a fool, but you could call me persona non persona. Officially speaking I do not exist. If that is the case then I guess you now have what we in the government term a "valid pretext for an excuse" not to listen to me. As I do not exist everybody else has already taken this VPFAE to ignore anything I might be prone to say. Regardless of who I may or may not be, whether I exist or whether you wish to pay any attention to me, the fact remains that this slip-up by the senator is going to cause quite a controversy.

$ $ $

So the question is: how is the office of the presidency of the United States of America responding to this embarrassment right now? What's the plan for handling the repercussions that are bound to come back to the political party both Gibson and the President belong to? For the moment this news has gone entirely undetected by the President and his closest advisors, as they are all holding a secret conference, with the preeminent members of the oil industry mainly. The President is trying hard to say something wise on the subject at hand but with the Vice President—or the Vice Pressy as the media has dubbed him—the Secretary of the Interior, a few nameless advisors who were behind the 1980's, and the members of the oil industry all jockeying for vocal dominance it's impossible to get a word in edgewise. *Imagine that,* he whispers to himself mentally, *I'm the leader of the free world and here I'm not even allowed to speak my piece.* In the end he really has nothing of any value to add as the whole conversation left his plane of understanding some time ago.

Sure, some of the auto people are represented, and some of the media conglomerates are present, and one or two smalltime consumer goods people such as the cheapo shoes guy, but this is mainly an energy affair. *They all want a piece of the pie,* he's thinking to himself. *These other government fellas might be the chefs but by gum I am the pie master,* he tells himself. *I dole out the pie. Me.*

"So the steps outlined in the energy policy notwithstanding, can we rely on the consumers to fall in line?" One of the many hungry corporate types, a guy by the name of Strauss, asks this after the briefing is concluded.

The Vice Pressy addresses them. "Our friends, the multimedia conglomerates—who do remember that it was our destruction of the antitrust laws in the 1980's which made them global conglomerates to begin with—will push our views and our views alone. I mean, to be honest, we all know that the current trend in reality television only goes so far!"

"What's that supposed to mean?" the faulty pump manufacturer asks.

"Well, come on, Reagan wasn't even the most popular President of the last fifty years, much less in the history of the nation. But after four years of us telling the people that through the mouth of our 'journalists' we had the voters literally eating out of the palms of our hands. Seriously."

"Listen, I'm all for that," Strauss says. "The only little thing is I'm not convinced it'll work...I mean, I know that it should work in principal, but are the people willing to go along with that type of thing? The inflation, I'm talking about. You can tell them whatever you want, but when they have less money they'll feel it, right?"

From the shadows one of the advisors speaks up. "There won't be any hiccups; it's a proven method. This is what we did twenty years ago and the operation went squeaky-clean. We are all guaranteed profit from this exercise; decreasing the value of the dollar means selling products for higher prices over-seas."

"And if any of our institutions were to be hit with substantial losses or succumb entirely during the process?"

"Don't worry. We can just use taxpayer money to bail you out."

"Hmm."

"Hmm."

"Hmm."

Wanting to take full advantage of this round of "hmm"—a thing that the President is actually an expert on, to his credit—he contributes the authoritative "*Hmmmmmmm...*" which gives everyone pause. Yes, this is taken as the signal from the man in charge that things are looking good from the Federal point of view, and that the presidency will do everything in its power to support the goals outlined here today.

"The taxpayer money?" the ambassador of flimsy pumps asks. "Can we rely on that being an ethical alternative?" For a second there is a grim silence as the men hesitate, looking around at each other before erupting into gales of laughter that rage out of control for minutes.

"You may not realize it, not being stationed in Washington, not being a Washingtonian, but everything is complimentary when it comes to the Federal government," the Secretary of the Interior says.

Wiping the tears of laughter from his eyes the President speaks up. "That was a good one, that was a good one. You just earned a good tax credit for the shoe industry pal."

The pump-meister greedily rubs his hands together with all the glee of a horde of rats while the other industry reps look on enviously.

Frustrated by all this talk the television rep clears his throat and jumps in with, "But what are we going to do about the viewership slump? I mean honestly. Can't you pass some law forcing people to watch our programming? Or maybe give 'education' tax breaks to families who force their kids to watch? We are down to a viewership of twenty-one million during prime time. That's less than a tenth of the populace."

One of the Commerce advisors, lower on the rungs than many but higher than most, sharing the rung with few, making him rather adept at runging or the art of rung politics—that is, a lower ranking person taking heat for those above his position—says, "You could try improving the quality of the shows, like the cable industry did." Again there is a dire moment of silence, a doubt-filled hesitation, before uproarious laughter again rules the meeting. The shadow advisors come to the conclusion that "silly mode" has been engaged, and the day's work should be adjourned until tomorrow.

For me to recount what happens next would be imprudent—due to matters of national security—and in fact it's simply too boring to bother with. Suffice it to say that over the course of the next seventy-two hours a "veritable shit storm" erupts over the senator's comments on *Hardline Nation*, while the policies that will shape the nation's destiny are devised behind closed doors.

$ $ $

During all of this a daring scientist has gotten fed up with the wall of silence the White House has erected around her. For months now she has been putting in requests through the various available channels to meet with the President of the United States and examine him with the tools of her discipline. This bold woman, Catherine Jauquesjourstd, has given in to an impulse to travel to the nation's capitol and force the government's hand: either they will grant her entry or they will tell her to shove off. She knows nothing of the secretive enclaves, nor does she care about the uproar in the press about the so-called "white-niggerism" controversy that started a few days ago.

Having arrived in the District yesterday she wasted no time early this morning, making sure that she was one of the first inside once the White House was made available to the public. It is now almost lunchtime and they still have not given her an answer. It's true, Catherine has been waiting for a long time now, but that's okay. It's given her time to consider whether or not head shrinking aboriginal tribes would be able to appreciate her line of work. As it stands they may be the only collection of people left who might not dismiss her out of hand. It is doubtful, after all, that Phrenology has been explained to such people. *Oh, what does that mean...such people? Everyone has been in contact with the outside world and been exposed to technology, modern advances, modern thinking. Yet so many choose to remain in the dark*, she ruefully adds in her internal debate.

A man happens by, distracted by a conversation with a subordinate, and stubs his toe on Catherine's equipment case. "My apologies miss," he is quick to say. This is General Perkin, a man of great influence within the Defense Department. He is what you'd call "old school" when it comes to his world view.

"It's okay, no harm done."

"Say, are you a doctor?" he asks, eying the bag. "Making a house call? I hope it's nothing serious."

"It is true, I am a doctor. Although my visit is not what you think. I'm just waiting to see the President."

"Oh! Then it is serious. I hope I'm not prying into anything sensitive, but we aren't talking about...a *grave* condition are we?" Both he and his subordinate have been taken with restrained concern.

"As I stated, this is not a serious medical matter or, in fact, a medical matter at all. My general field of study is the human mind."

"Right," he says, nodding, considering the implications and systematically ruling them out. "Like a psychologist."

"Correct."

"Right. But you said your general field of study. What about your specific field of study?"

Did the Administration send this military guy out to interrogate her? To scare her? Well, Catherine decides she will not give them the satisfaction. "The truth of the matter is that I am a Phrenologist."

The General has himself a good laugh. "What, the Commander-In-Chief needed an emergency hat-fitting?" He and the subordinate continue chuckling, although the subordinate has no grasp on what it means to be a phrenologist—possibly something to do with Scientology? It takes a few moments for them to realize that she is serious. "You...you really are one of those skull-mappers?"

"To put it crudely."

Perkin adjusts his belt. "Now, I've never heard of phrenologists making house calls before."

"Really, it is just a small research matter. I'm sure that you have more significant issues weighing on your mind today."

"I get it," Perkin chuckles. "Weighing on my mind. Right."

Catherine can't help feeling that a long day is only going to become longer, that a simple task such as measuring the President's head should not have to be so protracted. Already in her mind she is lining up all the arguments that Phrenology masters such as Gall and Bouts would use if they were at her side.

"Okay, if you were a shrink, I could understand that. Don't take this the wrong way, but a bona fide quack is all you are."

"The field of Psychoanalysis is completely subjective; that is, it is interpreted through the experience of the observer and therefore holds no solid scientific ground. I, however, am in the field of Phrenology which has a measurable, quantitative grounding, making it a completely objective science. And don't launch into something about how the Nazis tried to manipulate it to their advantage, that was Craniometry, not Phrenology."

The debate between Catherine and the General is shaping up to be a good one, but there are other matters, other events taking place that I would like to focus on...

$ $ $

In another portion of the White House a young fellow by the name of Billings is performing Herculean feats of juggling. He has been assigned the unenviable task of chaperoning the President of the United States of America around behind the scenes. The gouging and exhaust and megatons of red tape in the District of Columbia are a far cry from the comparatively relaxed pace of politics he knew in Wyoming. Sometimes, just sometimes, he wishes he were back home helping out at his father's carpentry business.

The President smacks his hands together as he does whenever his excitement gets the better of him. "Why does he get a nickname, huh? If he's the Vice Pressy then I'm going to be the Pressy."

"Hmm...uh, I don't know about that sir—"

"I don't see why not! I mean, what the heck is it coming to? He's not more popular than me, is he?!"

"No, no, good heavens no, the public doesn't even know what he looks like—"

"Well, I just don't see why he should get a nickname and I shouldn't. It's settled. I'm the Pressy from here on out. You tell 'em."

They continue down the hall, having finished with the issue of informal pet names. The President smoothes out his jacket and straightens his collar...nobody can tell him he can't be the Pressy if he wants to be.

That talk could have gone better, Billings tells himself. Unfortunately it won't make the next topic any easier for him to bring up. "There is another, more sensitive, matter that we need to address."

"Oh? By all means, let's address that sucker and put it in the mail," the President says, displaying the offhanded charm that got him into office.

"Yes, well, the recent polls and surveys have been indicating a troubling trend in public opinion. News of Gordon getting paid millions to endorse a product is not being well-received by the median, the mode, or the mean—"

The President interrupts with, "You know, that's the problem these days. People, our people, have been trained to be envious of those who work hard to get ahead."

"Ah, yes, that may well be true sir, but the consensus of the American people is that Gordon has—some may say—used his father's presidency to make money, thereby detracting from the reputation of the presidency."

"Well now, you and I both know that Aqua-Aqua is a fine product made right here in the US of A, I mean the spring water comes right out of the ground, it's the very lifeblood of this land. On top of all that I'm the Pressy, right? Not Gordon. People don't get us confused do they? I know I've still got my youthful good looks but come on, I hope this isn't going to be a problem..."

"No sir, I doubt that's the problem right now—"

"Humph. I wonder. Maybe we ought get some plastic surgery done on the boy so he doesn't look just like me. I mean, he has to look enough like me to be my son, of course, we can't have any rumors of that nature flying around. But still. People have to be able to tell which one of us is in charge. Or...hmm! Maybe, just maybe, we could use this, use it to our advantage, to my advantage."

"Sir, I'm not sure what you mean—"

"That is, if we dressed the same, do you think that I could sort of slink off and catch a little shuteye during some of these meetings? I mean, honestly, this stuff would bore the beard off the Lord Almighty himself. So come on, what do you think? Sounds like a good plan to me. Might even be a good decoy in case of assassins."

Deeply disturbed by this turn in the conversation Billings decides to sidestep the issue. "We'll have to give that one some thought, and perhaps confer on it at a later date when a more opportune time for discussion presents itself to be, uh, available."

"Right." Walking down hallways, down more and more hallways, the President muses. Seems like he's got his own personal mad scientist's test maze set up around him, only there is no exit, there is no lump of cheese waiting for him at the end. "Anything else on the agenda today? Anything out of the ordinary? Come on Billings, surprise me. Like, for instance, who was that woman with the glasses and the weird case waiting around out there? Some kind of journalist? No, no, hold on: starving kids. She's got a bunch of refugee kids that need feeding. Am I close? I've been working on that whole 'beta mind state' thing, building up my psychic prowess if you will."

"Well, the fact of the matter is that she's a, ah, phrenologist and is requesting an audience with you—"

"A phrenologist? Why didn't you say so, I've been needing to refill some of these prescriptions." The President pats down his pockets, wondering what he did with those darn prescriptions; why does his groin continue to itch, what did his wife's ass look like five years ago?

"Um, well sir, I believe you will find that what you are thinking of is a pharmacologist while what we are dealing with, on the other hand, is a phrenologist..." He smiles at the President but realizes that the message is still lost, entirely lost. "One of those who practices the debunked discipline of taking measurements of human skulls in the attempt to deduce the intangible facets a person possesses as an individual." He smiles again, nodding this time, confident that the content of his words was not lost on the leader of the nation.

"Debunked? What the heck, let's bunk that sucker up again! So she wants to measure my head, huh? I think that's a capital idea. She can put it in the record books along with Julius Caesar and Napoleon and Mohammed Ali. Think she'll fill these while she's at it?" the President asks, extending a handful of prescriptions for vitamins that could be purchased over the counter but, well, that doesn't seem official enough does it?

"No, no sir, no I don't think so, not really. Besides, I think the whole thing may just be a waste of your time. There's the McClemmet Bill to address—"

"Oh, hogwash. I always have time to bunk a phrenacologist. That reminds me, did you put in the request for bunk beds? I hear the kids want to have some friends over. By the way, why is she requesting an audience? This phrenacologist that is. Is the meeting going to be televised?"

It takes Billings a second to process this statement and understand it fully. "No sir, that's not what I meant." They stand in silence for a moment, Billings considering the various alternatives facing his attempt to explain without making his boss seem like a dunce. The President, meanwhile, is trying to recall the names of the seven elves that go mining for cookies every day, trudging off to work singing their song and leaving Rapunzel all alone....no, Rapunzel was the wife of Rumpelstiltskin, that guy who slept for a hundred years. But the President is sure, positive, that the elves do mine for cookies in that tree stump and sell them to passersby from a cute little window in the side of the stump. *Must've been a redwood*, the President muses. *Wasn't that based on a true story? A bunch of inbreds living in the foothills of California? Could be movie-of-the-week material.*

Billings clears his throat and gestures to his clipboard, which is holding the itinerary for the day. "Things are rather, you know, booked today sir. But don't worry, we'll get you that meeting with the, ah, phrenologist."

"With an audience?"

"We'll work on that one sir. While we're taking care of the political business of the day I can arrange to have these prescriptions filled."

"Would you now? That's a boy!" He gleefully hands the papers over to his less-than-enthused subordinate. "Oh yeah, another thing..."

$ $ $

A short while later Catherine is still in the same place, growing impatient, continuing to argue with the war hawk. Thankfully she spies the same young man she spoke with earlier as he enters and approaches her, hopefully bringing some official word with him.

General Perkin also notices that little pansy heading his way and decides to shove off, wanting no part of a meeting with both a sissy and a feminist. "All right Miss, sorry to get your panties all tied up in a knot but I've got to run. I have important things to do such as, you know, maintaining the most powerful democracy the world has ever seen."

"It is a democracy? I hadn't noticed. By the way, you can call me Ms. or Ma'am, whichever you prefer. And I too must apologize because it seems that I have gotten your loin cloth all tied in a knot."

"Ha ha," the General says, without humor, before departing.

Catherine tries her best not to waste any more thought on the war hawk and just focus on the task at hand. The way Billings is wringing his hands as he approaches is not comforting to her, quite the opposite; she begins to gather her belongings, positive that the hours of waiting have been fruitless. Catherine is used to the fact that being a master of her discipline means mandatory expulsion from most "reputable" institutions.

"Pardon the delay," Billings says as he draws near. "I hope that I have not inconvenienced you. Do you need to get somewhere?"

"No, no," Catherine says, suddenly feeling foolish for starting her retreat so soon. "Have you received any word on whether the President will see me?"

"Yes, Ms. Jauquesjourstd, I have spoken with the President directly and he has expressed his explicit interest in—and support of—your research."

"What? I mean, thanks, I am very grateful for this opportunity."

"There is a drawback, however, in that certain unpredictables have converged in such a way that he will be indisposed for the duration of the day, most likely. We do have an alternate plan that you may find more than suitable." Already he's fingering a name tag with "Hawkshurst/SC Clearance" written on it.

I can't blame him for the tricks that phonetics play on the human mind.

"An alternative?" Catherine muses, back on guard. "I can examine the busts of the former Presidents, right? Is that what you're trying to tell me?"

"No, not at all Ms. Jauquesjourstd." He is uncomfortable with the "other thing" the President wanted of him, but perhaps it will provide enough of a distraction or simply scare the researcher off completely. "While we are waiting to set up a time for you to meet directly with the President you may, in the meantime, examine the other members of his family."

"That is unexpected. I would have thought he wouldn't want anything to do with this, if I may be perfectly blunt."

"As it turns out he is very excited by the opportunity to participate in a scientific undertaking and, in fact, wished to have his family included to provide the most thorough record possible. And, if you wish, you may also examine the busts of the former presidents of the United States."

She explains that such will not be necessary and thanks Billings for the opportunity to examine the First Family. When pressed on the issue of a firm date for meeting with the leader he is a bit too slippery for her liking, but she'll just have to settle for what they allow her. "So when may I begin?"

"It so happens that the President's daughter, Bethany, is here at the White House right this minute, without any obligations for the remainder of the day. If you so desire you may start immediately." That's how things get set in motion.

So Catherine is entering the room now, confused as to why she should want to examine the first daughter's head, confused as to why security refused to escort her—a stranger meeting with the First Daughter—and, stumbling in the dark, she flips on a light switch thinking the girl isn't even there at all. What the lights reveal are three young women—one of them being Bethany—next to nude on a plush, disordered bed wearing only hats, shoes, and various accessories, with a five-foot python or anaconda loose on the floor and about twelve packs worth of playing cards strewn all over. Some shoplifted lingerie hangs from the antique dresser, with a number of shoplifted modems and stolen hubcaps. On the vanity are two plastic bags containing what looks to be four kilos of cocaine and next to that is an empty milk jug filled with dried mushrooms, with a tray of sugar cubes between them. A skinned rat dangles overhead from the very center of the ceiling and this seems to agitate the snake even more than it bothers Catherine. A pair of young black boys, impoverished and no more than seven or eight years of age, huddle in the corner afraid to move. The girls on the bed are casually posed, not sexually, just sort of lounging on each other, high as a kite, and one of the two no-names is using a saw to hack through a renegade fingernail that looks at least eight inches in length. Why should Catherine want to examine the First Daughter's head, indeed?

Bethany is as startled as anyone present and thinks to herself, *Hmm, what a delish dish...I wonder how she got in here?* It does not occur to Bethany in her state of higher consciousness that maybe, just maybe, she forgot to lock the door. Seeing that Catherine left the door slightly ajar and is turning to it now, as if she intends to leave, Bethany scoops up the remote. Zap, just like that, the door swings shut of its own accord.

"Da-aa-amn Bethy baby, that is some fly-ass shit..." the raven-haired girl says, ogling over the remote control as if it's a Martian artifact.

"No shit baby, that's bombalicious, maxin' and taxin'..." the bleached blonde agrees.

Bethany says nothing, her head just lolling about under its own power while she considers this newcomer.

"I just want to leave," Catherine says, trying not to look at them, cursing herself for getting involved in this family's messed-up life. "I don't want to know what's going on. Just unlock that door and I'll be on my way." Then, "I won't say a thing about any of...this, to anybody."

"Oh?" Bethany laughs. "What is 'this' anyways? What's that supposed to mean?"

"Just, um, anything that you wouldn't want people to be privy to, to know about. I won't tell anyone. Our secret."

"Mmm. Our secret..."

"Your secret."

The girls laugh now and for some reason the boys pressing themselves into the corner cringe at the sound. The snake is aware of Catherine's presence but keeps its distance. The rat? Twirling slightly due to the current provided by the ventilation system. Bethany catches the phrenologist eyeing the mountain of controlled substances. "Go ahead, help yourself. It's on—" Bethany stops here, unable to control a laughing jag. "—it's on the house!" Seeing that the woman makes no move, does not even acknowledge the offer, she feels the need to exert more hospitality. "Come on, it's free, take some, what do I care? I insist lady. Don't you know? Everything's complimentary here."

"Ooh, big words Bethany!" the fake blonde cackles.

It can be said, quite understandably, that Catherine is a bit trepidatious here, having not been in this kind of situation before. The doorknob won't turn and these girls are obviously insane on whatever chemicals they've indulged in. What's more is she could easily jeopardize herself by mistepping and making the wrong people upset. Would the Powers That Be really want a witness to this debauchery running around like a loose cannon?

The dark-haired girl plucks at one of Bethany's many necklaces, letting it slap against the area between the first daughter's breasts repeatedly while staring at Catherine with what can only be called an air of witlessness. The blonde finally saws off her fingernail. All the other nails are on the long side but she has severed this one just past the finger tip, a fact that is only now dawning on her, and she is about ready to go berserk at the thought of unsymmetrical fingernails. Catherine is fingering her equipment case, wondering if there are suitable objects for self defense contained within.

On the floor the serpent snaps at a stray cricket. *Grave condition, indeed.* Now Catherine knows why phrenologists never make house-calls. She'd like to slap that stupid general right about now.

$ $ $

While Catherine is busy coping with her situation Billings has herded the President to a meeting, just another in an unending torrent of meetings and pow-wows. The President is contemplating his earlier discussion with Billings instead of listening to these expert folks. Why can't they just make a little cut here, a little snip there, and make Gordon look just like him? The President could be out buying magazines or chopping wood or getting rid of weeds on his property, instead of being stuck in another dreary chamber.

This particular presentation is all about the role of the Coast Guard as a contingency in the event of martial law resulting from either an invasion of Greys or the sighting of the Antichrist, whichever may occur first. The President has been briefed on it all during the travel time to this subterranean computer simulation chamber. Of course, that was only a walk down a hallway, a ride down an elevator, and a long stroll through several corridors. The Antichrist, well, the President is more than knowledgable on the subject. About Greys, on that front he isn't too clear, but he'll just nod and say something commanding as he usually does, or comment about commitment, his commitment to the act of being committed. That should do the trick.

The dozens of screens throughout the chamber—the little ones at the stations of the minions and the medium sized ones at the stations of the boss men, accompanied by the big boy straight ahead—all spring to life with the same string of initialization code and start-up commands. The President leans in close to Billings and, in his best "computer-generated voice" whispers, "*Would-you-like-to-play-a-game?*"

Billings chuckles. "Very good sir." His boss never passes up the opportunity for a good *War Games* joke. General Perkin overhears Billings' voice and gives him a this-is-serious-business stare.

Without warning a huge computer-generated map of the People's Republic of China slams into view on every monitor, followed seconds later by an enormous CGI of the United States descending from the top of the screen. What happens next, shockingly, is that the United States thrusts the Florida Peninsula into the Yellow River and China proclaims: "Me love you long time! Me love you long time!" The act continues and so does the voice, garnering laughs and chuckles all around, despite the fact that it is slightly embarrassing to the computer nerds.

"All right," Pibbles, the director of the project, says while stepping forward. "I'm confiscating this right now. Hand it over." One of the techs hastily shuts down the program, stammering something about not understanding how it was triggered, or better yet where it came from, and hands a compact disk over to Pibbles. "Mr. President, you have my most sincere apologies—"

"No, no," the President says with a wave of his hand, "no harm done. I thought it was kinda funny myself." He laughs lightly and the computer squad follows are relieved at his unexpected understanding. "As a matter of fact I have a pretty good Chinaman joke if you guys want to hear it—"

"Ah, sir," Billings says, scrutinizing his watch for all he's worth, "we really are on the tightest of schedules today. Perhaps, Mr. Pibbly—"

"It's Pibbles—"

"—yes, Pibbles, if you could just sort of skip the intro and get things into full swing here, there have been, well, a lot of unexpected situations arising that the President needs to address. You understand."

"Of course," Pibbles states curtly.

"And I'll hold onto that disk, for safe keeping," Billings says, obviously confident in his position with the new administration. Pibbles clears his throat, looks around, and without being too hesitant hands the disk over to this kid, this upstart who has the ear of the most powerful man in the world. A compact disk, a job, the jobs of everyone in the department, why not hand it all over? As they say: *everything is complimentary here*. And what you want to avoid, if you are working at the White House, is working yourself into a grave position as the quickest remedy is often a swing of the axe.

Pibbles sighs. "Okay people. You heard the man. Get this show underway, ASAP."

The attention shifts once again to the monitors, this time only displaying a calm collection of data pertaining to the depth of the Coast Guard reserves, the specs on the spacecraft the Greys are purported to be using these days, the kinetic force of one ton of brimstone dropped from the upper stratosphere, etc. As the lights dim and the experts begin to deliver their reports Billings feels a wave of self admiration. It is at this time that he notices the President is watching him with a "way to go" expression. The President even does some mock muscle flexing, causing Billings to laugh. Even though Billings kept it quiet Perkins turns and glares at him again, obviously feeling that the young man is not up to military snuff. Can Billings help it if his boss likes to monkey around?

$ $ $

That evening, after Catherine extricates herself from a hairy situation with seven sets of measurements—yes, Bethany insisted that she even measure the young boys and the animals—after Billings has scampered away to his ridiculously priced apartment in Alexandria, after Senator Gibson's widely disregarded apology earlier in the day...it is time for the President to meet with his psychic advisor.

The family psychic is seated at the table, her hands fluttering, the room already abuzz with that certain mystique she imbues in her surroundings, in her every utterance and motion. She has not one but two crystal balls—one to either side—and the tarot cards are at rest before her. Aside from the chicken bones, the pot of cinders, the Ouija board, the crow's foot, the infant skull—not from an abortion, she has assured them—the smoldering incense, the assorted roots known for their magikal properties, and the elaborate multicolored candles, the rest of the table perfectly clear.

The First Lady and the President hold hands under the table, fearful of letting their nervousness show in case the spirits are watching. He is worried about his toenails; they've been yellowing lately. She is concerned about the long sleepless nights that have plagued her since the First Family moved into the executive mansion.

Jirina is worried that they will begin to favor that Mrs. Cleopatra lady who has been getting so popular...as if she has any connection to the Egyptians! This is going to test her repertoire of skills. Without warning something comes to her, a simple message, an insidiously simple message. Gravely Jirina states, "*They're here.*"

The President and his wife look to each other in the full thrall of suspense. "What can that mean?" he whispers, lightly pounding his fist on the table. "I mean...what can it mean?"

A shriek bursts from Jirina now as she claws at her face, mortified, rocking back and forth while the first couple brace themselves on each other, fright dominating their breathing, their expressions. Jirina wails and wails, then suddenly, shockingly: silence! Her head lowers...has she been possessed? Has the seer been overcome? Slowly, *spookily* for lack of a better description in the President's mind, Jirina's head rises, her air foreboding, her eyes rolled up exposing only the whites.

"No!" the First Lady says, unable to restrain herself any longer.

"Don't tell me—not a—a—a poltergeist!"

"Yes!" Jirina shouts. "A poltergeist! A former occupant of this world, now a denizen of the afterlife! Someone who spent time here in the White House, yes!"

"A *denizen* of the *afterlife?*" the President repeats, the horror of the unknown casting its shadow over him.

"Yes...an interloper originating from the darkest depths of the nether regions...the border worlds of purgatory...not living, but not entirely dead...*we love them like we love decay*....no! Don't say that! *Yes! Consume!* No, don't listen to them! Pray! Pray now!"

Hearing Jirina's voice alternate back and fourth between the wholesome prophetess of this world and evil dead of another realm has to be even more frightening than those live debates last fall. The First Couple comply with Jirina's instructions immediately; they learned long ago never to question supernatural matters. While they pray earnestly, in silence, with heads bowed and the hair on the backs of their necks at full attention, Jirina undertakes an involved ritual involving a healthy quantity of smoke, ashes, and the roots. When she finishes she grips the crystal balls with unnecessary vigor, her arms rigid as iron, like a captain at the helm in the throes of a hurricane.

"Whom have you offended?!" Jirina shouts, startling the couple out of their spiritual reveries.

"I...I don't know..." the First Lady blurts. Desperate for an answer she turns on her husband. "Did you offend somebody? Was it you? I don't think I offended anybody!"

"Well don't look at me hon, I'm not the one who painted the Jefferson room that God-awful shocking pink."

"Oh!" That had totally escaped her mind. "I...I mean...do you think that did it?"

Jirina shakes her head with grim intensity. "You cannot rush matters involving the spirit world. The vast eternal darkness is a timeless void full of squirming hordes intent on nothing but making the living suffer. To them time has no meaning." Obviously it would not be to Jirina's advantage for this to be an issue which can be resolved in only one session. "We may have to combat these forsaken forces of ferocious darkness for some time to come."

"I—I didn't mean it, I—I—I just like pink is all," the First Lady stammers.

"Say no more dear," Jirina says, her eyes darting about as she tries to root out the source of psychic disturbance. "It could be that some practitioner of black magik has directed these forces against you, perhaps a political rival or ill-wishers from enemy governments. Perhaps...yes, perhaps this relates to a tragedy that occurred here in the past, before your time. Possibly even before the construction of this mortal structure. Only time will tell."

"But," the President blurts, "I thought time doesn't mean anything to these folks?"

"To the brigands of the afterlife, perhaps, but we may use time to our advantage Mr. President. I feel that the three of us, working together, with the grace of the Lord, may be able to conquer the spirits who oppose us."

$ $ $

While the First Couple chews that proposition over a member of the Secret Service escorts our phrenologist through the White House. Unfortunately for Catherine she has yet to make it out of this crazy place. Members of The Administration ran into her earlier, as she was leaving, and insisted that she have a visit with the President's son. Of course Catherine respectfully declined but she has discovered it is not so easy as all that. Now, outside of Gordon's door, she is faced with the horror of the unknown. "Please," the man says, gesturing toward the door.

Catherine hesitates here as the memories of her last visit with the First Family come to her. A part of her that she would gladly deny is anxious to go through the door, find what is on the other side, probe it and measure it with her instruments, get to the root of the workings of a presidential family's psychological composition.

He clears his throat and adds, "We insist."

What is that supposed to mean? "I would feel more comfortable if you would accompany me—"

"Sorry ma'am but we're on strict orders not to enter the private rooms of the First Children unless it is an emergency situation." The man looks at his watch, growing impatient, then receives a call on his cell phone informing him of a rockslide in New Mexico that buried a school bus filled with children. "A situation has developed ma'am, but I trust you can handle the rest. Good evening," he says, and the man races off hoping to snag pictures of the carnage for his private collection.

With her keeper wandering away to who-knows-what Catherine feels a sense of relief, for only the shortest amount of time because she hears, to her dismay, the voices of the war hawk and his underlings approaching from around the corner. With nowhere else to go she bolts into the First Son's room, no longer dwelling on what may be waiting for her. Huddled in the darkness just inside the room this is what Catherine sees:

The First Son, his chest and teeth brutally bared; Gordon is illuminated by an extreme, hateful blue strobe light resting on the floor; lit from below creepy shadows detail his every tensed muscle, his every distended vein, as he stands snarling, screeching, his hunter's eyes focused on some phantasmal prey in the outlying darkness of his room. Gordon's feet are far apart, as if he has assumed some wide martial arts stance, his quivering arms rigidly pointing down, his fists turned inwards so that the knuckles are pressed together. This is disturbing enough. The shocker is that his two pals, Blinky and some jock, are furiously working the handles of two pumps which shoot what looks to be water into his bloodstream through two enormous needles. The network of tortured blood vessels that weaves a horrible texture over Gordon's skin is so pronounced that it casts shadows of its own in the depressed flicker.

Catherine instantly slips through the door, praying to whatever benevolent force looks down on water addiction that those three insane boys don't see her.

"So, so, so...we meet again. What is it this time little lady?" General Perkin, again, like the cat that always jumps out of the closet in a horror movie. After the day's events Catherine feels as though she is trapped in a haunted house.

$ $ $

The debate over the validity of Phrenology as a science has already been visited, so I would rather shift back to the Commander-in-Chief. He and his wife are storming into their bedroom deeply rattled by the night's revelations. "We've got to put an end to these *denizens!*" he proclaims, smashing his hands together. "Damn these damn *denizens*, we won't have it. No! I don't care if it is Lincoln or Hubert Humphrey. I don't care if it's every single mistress that ever traipsed through here. Wait a minute. Hmm. Well, that could be interesting, on the other hand..."

"Hello? Hello?" The First Lady has put herself through to Secret Service Command. "This is—oh, you know damn well who this is! I want to know about something I heard once. Isn't there a psy-thing? Para-Ops? Yes, I think that's it! I want a swarm of Psi-Ops people up here on the double."

"You know, they say—I've heard this anyway—that ghost lovers are the best..."

"What do you mean there is no such thing? I thought we even had a resident Para-Ops agent, one assigned to us specifically!"

"Hmm. No, no. What am I thinking? We must be talking major scary stuff here. *Beaucoup* scary stuff. Jirina never gets like that. I better get my game face on for these 'denizens'...that's what I'm gonna do!"

"Everybody was afraid...what? Did I just hear you correctly? Everybody thought these psychic agents would figure out that they lied on their tax returns?! Are you serious? Are you even listening to yourself? Why, that is just simply ludicrous!"

"Beaucoup...beaucoup..."

"What do you mean there's another call?"

"Damn...so you ghosts are watching me on the john, huh?! What kind of perverts are you! You should be ashamed!"

"Hello? Hello?!" While the First Lady slams the receiver the President is snatching randomly at the air itself, unsuccessful in his attempts at barehanded ghostbusting. "Oh, what are you doing now? Stop that. Stop that!"

"I'll wrangle these suckers one way or another sugar-pie, just you wait and see."

"Sugar-pie?"

"That's right. Since I came to D.C. I'm the pie meister, and if that's the case you've got to be my sugar-pie..."

Watching him attacking the air like a man besieged by hornets, with her hands on her hips, the First lady is unsure what to make of the man she decided to share her life with. "I'll be in the little girl's room."

"Wait!" he cries. "Don't use the bathroom. It's not safe. Use, um, why don't you try the kitchen?"

"You are deranged! What has come over you?"

"It's just that, well, you know...how do I put this politely...they can, um, the denizens..." He pauses to cup his hands over his mouth and whisper, "They watch us doing our business."

"Oh Lord!" she exclaims, throwing her hands up in the air. "Well if they watch me pee in there they can see me anywhere, now can't they?"

The thought makes the President jump back, suddenly afraid...very afraid.

$ $ $

Over the next two days there are many other things to fear, most of which go unnoticed and are totally irrelevant, or classified, so let's look at what the media would have us fear. After the conservative elements recoup and let their think tank go to work the stage is set. The President and his core advisors are gathered in a lounge on the premises of the White House—which is, as far as the President is concerned, still very much alive with those afterlife denizens—to watch the fruits of their labors. It is only slightly disconcerting that the Vice President has been absent the last couple days, but they have assured the President that he is just having a minor medical exam done.

The lunch hour news brings the large-screen television to life. Gibson's voice buzzes through the speakers even, calm, overly-practiced at not sounding practiced. In his attempt to conceal that everything he is about to say has been scripted the senator loses his regional inflection and mannerisms, which is a dead giveaway that some staff member drafted up these comments. "People say, 'Oh well now, that Gibson fella, he's a good 'ol boy but darn if he ain't a black-hater...that Gibson, he hates the black folk' and blah blah blah, on they go. What people don't know about me, what people don't care to understand about me, is that I am a man who is not a black-hater but is a lover of...I love things, different, differing things, in equal...proportions, so you can say, equal and different, I am a lover of things and people proportionally. I love America! I love the fact that you can have different viewpoints and opinions and have the diversity of, say, he comes from Scotland and he comes from England, and that's all right with me. So when I value all members of our society how can I be considered one of these 'hating' people?"

Gibson is standing in front of his residence, roughly ten feet away from a young Hispanic boy, his incessant smile full of pride in his actions. "Why I done adopted myself one of these Americans of divergent ethnicity, if you will—and I will—and here I say is the evidence which is self-evident, so to speak, so the point speaks for itself without defeating itself, the point is not defeating itself and remains undefeated, I think. Quite clearly what we have here is me, Jefferson Alan Gibson, bringing into my home an African American child." Some flashbulbs go off as he poses in his triumphant moment of bridging the racial divide which he helped to open.

"Sir, this boy is Spanish," one of the reporters states.

"'Scuse me?"

"Spanish, Senator Gibson. The boy, he's, ah...Spanish?"

On hearing this a second time Gibson takes a few steps closer to the youngster, scrutinising him at length. "No. You don't say? Well that's got to be the brownest little Spaniard this side of Koon County!" He laughs playfully at his own joke, not waiting for anyone else to laugh first.

A close-up of the child reveals that he is lost in what is happening to him, around him, the recent life-altering events still not taking hold in his mind, nor is the misfortune of who has adopted him registering. We cut to a shot of Gibson and the boy sitting at a small table on the porch, the man offering a peeled banana and the boy just staring at it.

"I've made sure to include all the comforts of home that his kind would be accustomed to," Gibson says while using the peeled banana as a pointer to emphasize his words. "I've undertaken a thorough study of the African American culture."

"But isn't he Spanish, Senator Gibson?"

The politician pauses. "We can argue the vagaries of man's origin back and forth all day, partner."

"Is he or is he not Spanish? It's a simple question."

Obviously flustered Gibson brandishes the banana. "Well now! I take umbrage at this line of questioning." That's all anybody needs to see. One of the advisors has to get up and switch the television off since that Billings kid is off on some errand.

"Boys," the Press Secretary says, "We are screwed."

"Yeah, well, sure that was pretty bad and all, PR-wise, and sure, as you pointed out earlier today, the polls are falling like whore's drawers, but I'll tell you what fellas, I've hatched a brainchild." The President settles back in his seat in preparation to release his genius; he fails to notice that the others are not comforted by his statement. "It's no secret guys. I mean, come on. We all know how things went down so let's not lie to each other here. I had my price. Thirty mil, well, that's not a price just anybody can pay, nor is it a price that just anybody can ask for. And if I have a price I'll be damned if those same people criticizing it don't have their own price. Thirty mil? Is that something we have at our fingertips, just laying around collecting dust? You know it, that much and more, probably ten or a hundred times more than that. But who are all these people? Do they deserve as much as the President of the United States of America? Shucks no! Least not in my opinion, and if you differ then, please guys, keep it to yourselves." That gets them chuckling again. "I've been thinking hard on it. You put a hundred-thousand of these folks together and you might get yourself the worth of a guy in my position. Last time I checked the calculator that's

$300 per person, for everybody who paid taxes let's say. Now how about that? Slip 'em three big ones through the mail, from the IRS say, and they'll fall in line, I'd stake my reputation on it."

The advisors are sitting around in a shell-shocked circle, bug-eyed, unable to believe the brilliant scheme they just heard actually came from the man fronting the government. One of them asks, "How fast can we swing this? Can it happen tomorrow? As an emergency measure I mean, we've got to push this right now as an emergency measure to stave off some kind of 'impending economic disaster.'"

"Economic disaster?" another asks. "But that isn't scheduled until next year. I mean, you've got to do a lot of prep work to sell people on that."

"No, no, we're not actually having the economic disaster, we're just telling them that. Sure, it's a little stagnant, but it's not a disaster yet, not until we give the say so. I'm just providing a VPFAE here."

"Ah," they all say in unison.

The Secretary of Commerce clears his throat. "In that case I don't see why it can't happen. Let's do this thing. A $300 'tax credit' to get voters back in our pocket."

They all laugh and high-five, and at long last the President feels like one of the guys. Finally things are falling together.

$ $ $

In other parts of the White House things are in the process of falling apart. Case in point: two ladies having a surprisingly pleasant chat in one of the private rooms. Tea and light snacks have been delivered and even partially consumed. Catherine is not sure why she returned for a second helping but her research is more important than her comfort level. The fleeting emotional distress of the individual is nothing when compared to the accomplishments of science, which are timeless. That's her thinking anyhow. Then there is the First Lady.

Her mood is best described as buoyant. After years of deterioration...well, this is embarrassing, but I guess I've gone this far haven't I? After years of deterioration the First Couple's sex life has been invigorated. Or, maybe resuscitated is a better word to describe it. While the instruments are being fit at her temples, at the back of her skull, the First Lady is lost in thought. The whole thing has been so daring lately, that's what did the trick. The thought of spectral voyeurs at first terrified her, but when she slipped into bed the prospect grew more and more enticing. She isn't sure if she's one of those people, those *exhibitionist* people, oh heaven forbid! No, no, she just needs to have an audience to get her thrills.

Gordon barges in with his baggy pants and oversized sweater, chugging away on a forty-ounce Aqua-Aqua. "Oh, hey, what up Moms. I didn't know you were in here."

"Can't you call me Mother?" the First Lady distractedly replies. She's too busy making a mental note to cancel their next appointment with Jirina. "What's so hard about the word 'mother?'"

"Dads don't mind," Gordon says between sips. "Hey, don't I know you from somewhere?"

Catherine has been doing her best to keep her face hidden from the kid. "No, I don't believe we have ever met."

"Oh, how rude of me! Gordy honey, this is Ms. Jauquesjourstd. She's a scientist here to do a little research. It's for the good of humankind."

"Really?" Gordon sneers. "Looks like some kind of Frankenstein operation."

"Gordy!"

"It's okay," Catherine says, hoping to get things smoothed out so she can leave as quickly as possible.

"Moms. Why do you have to call me that? Especially in front of chicks. That's so not cool."

"How dare you talk that way Gordon! This is a highly educated woman, not some 'chick,' so mind your manners, and your mother."

While mother and son continue to go at it Catherine works at a steady pace. She ponders whether or not she has ever been referred to as a chick before. There is no conclusive answer as she can't have possibly been in the presence of every conversation about her.

"Tell me, Catherine—if I may call you Catherine—how did my son stack up? He has a Harvard-grade skull I'm hoping."

"Actually we don't have a ranking system such as that in place. Regardless, I have not had the chance to examine Gordon."

"Oh? You haven't? Gordy—Gordon—be a dear and set aside some time to let Ms. Jauquesjourstd phrenitise you."

"So you wanna measure me, huh lady? I don't know. That contraption looks like some kind of giant nut cracker."

"Gordon—"

"Hey, hey, I'm just kidding. Look, I'll be around for a little bit so why don't we just get this out of the way."

"Sounds good to me," Catherine says.

All this talk is killing the First Lady's mood, so it is time for her to show some initiative and change the topic. "So, doctor...I suppose you've heard tale of the hauntings here at our humble home? Well, to lay the rumors to rest, I can tell you first hand that they are the truth."

While his mother launches into a subject which is entirely old-hat to him Gordon waits impatiently, his agitation increasing proportionately as he takes sip after sip of the water. For real, he'd rather be chatting this chick up on the topic of his car collection, his phat gear, the origins of "phat" as prison slang—Pretty Hot And Tempting—a little-known fact that always makes him come off like a guru. He'd do anything to shut the old lady up right now. What about his scheme to get water coolers installed in every room of the White House? It would be a dream come true. The fact that he is sweating in a comfortable room temperature is normal for him. The fact that all his senses are going haywire is also normal for him.

As it turns out the rest of Catherine's visit is mercifully mundane. She gathers her data from the field, along with dozens of White House ghost stories, and heads home for the day. The Administration still refuses to set a definitive time for a meeting with the President himself. In the ever-evolving case of the senator who could not keep his mouth shut Gibson's office has sent out three press releases in the last twenty-four hours. None has managed to sway public opinion. Otherwise, the day is uneventful.

$ $ $

When the people wake and go about their lives the next day things are quite different. It is the day that the "white-niggerism" backlash and the President's sliding approval ratings will be defeated with a single blow. The Administration has been abuzz all day long after the successful push of their "emergency measures" regarding the national bribe...that is, the national economic relief. While nobody bought the President's claims of impending economic failure during his campaign—hardly a promising selling point for a politician—and the public does not feel the situation is desperate yet, the fact that mild recession caused by his claims has become a reality, giving him enough political power to swing the deal. Anybody lost yet?

While the President is busy in the prep room getting his make-up applied for the cameras and memorizing his lines, his flock of advisors is growing concerned. The visual aids for the press conference are nowhere to be found. After conferring with the graphics people it has become apparent that they did in fact deliver the disk of CGI material on time this morning to the office of the top presidential aid. That means Billings, and the men corner him backstage.

"I am not quite sure what you are asking," Billings says, stepping carefully here.

"We leave this one small detail to you and what we get is chaos at T-minus thirty minutes..."

"Well—"

"Young man, we have an advanced monitor system out there—one of the most advanced mind you—but if the President goes to use it and nothing happens that equipment might as well be a horse's ass. Those three dozen reporters out there are going to eat the President alive. They're just waiting for the chance. Are you trying to give them the chance?"

"No, no, I—"

"You do have the presentation ready?"

"Sure, sure, I was out this morning but they delivered it to my office. I saw it on the desk, it's a compact disk so you can't miss it."

As they send an errand girl bouncing on her way the Secretary of the Interior states, "What we need right now is for things to be moving like clockwork, not slopwork. With that whole debacle Gibson orchestrated yesterday we need this to be an unparalleled success. Things are getting off to an inauspicious start though..."

Without the President in attendance to shield him Billings feels suddenly very naked. Yes, he has become a very naked small man in a wilderness inhabited by giants. He watches the comings and goings of junior staff members nervously for signs of the disk being delivered. With only ten minutes to spare it reaches its final destination and he can breath easily at last. The rest of the day will be a piece of cake and a PR coup.

The President himself is feeling quite confident. He's prepared to get out there and show the nation what he's all about. "Remember, this one is going to be live," a television guy explains. That may have even been the director. The important thing is that the President gets his game face on. This is it. Do or die time. The moment to shift the tide back in their direction.

And so, minutes later, he finds himself addressing the press as if this is a business-as-usual affair, kicking things off with the typical rhetoric about education. "People are complaining that their children are not able to make it over the bar that the system has set up. As the Pressy I make the solemn pledge to take all of our nation's children to the bar."

In the midst of the snickers a reporter manages to ask, "But, Mr. President, don't you feel that we ought to *raise* the bar?"

"If we do that, how are people going to drink?" This comment draws chuckles all around, good-natured ones this time, not derisive, and realizing that he's "made a funny" the President pushes onward with it. "It'll be bad for business. If that happens from raising the bar then we'll have to lower the liquor tax and the whole surplus could get botched up in the process, which," he pauses to chuckle a bit himself, "brings me to my next point fellas. And that is the economy." The many advisors and officials in attendance inwardly applaud the deft use of charisma and the brilliant segue, a skill at which their leader excels.

"The surplus of the nation. What are we going to do with it? What should be done? These are the questions that I have been asked time and time again, as well as my advisors and supporters, and they are the questions which we have been asking ourselves as well. It takes a lot of soul searching on the part of a leader, a nation's leader, to decide what is best for his people. Well, I am here today to tell you that I've done just that. I have been to the wilderness and come back a wiser man for it." Okay, that last sentence was an improvisation on his part. "In light of the looming economic woes which we are presented with, which nobody could predict, we are faced with few alternatives. Unfortunately the previous administration did not take appropriate measures to ensure the stability of the economy, did not take measures to ensure economic growths for all American citizens. As I have always said I am a man of action and I firmly believe, in my heart, that this characteristic is what inspired the people to elect me in the first place. I have arrived in Washington to get things done, to make things happen, and one of those happenings is about to happen." He turns with regal flair to face the high-tech monitor set up about ten feet to his right. "Ladies and gentlemen, I give you the first moment that I, as forty-third President of the United States, humbly hope to be remembered for, the first of many such moments."

The reporters put their comments about giving citizens economic growths on hold, politely awaiting the video presentation. As the President just said, this will be the moment he is remembered for: a CGI of China appears at the bottom of the screen, much to the consternation of the staff members who are in a position to see it. While China waits at the bottom of the screen the United States begins to descend from above...

"Oh God no—" Billings says aloud, drawing surprised looks. He attempts to give the "kill it" signal as inconspicuously as possible but the effort goes unnoticed by the staff members nearest the monitor.

Florida is diving for the Yellow River...

"Hmm, now what you see here is—is the global economy—yes, the trade deals and deficits between the esteemed people of China and America. This is how we negotiated with China and, uh, the results..."

Just as the President finishes speaking Florida stabs China, again and again causing pleasured moans to blast from the speakers, accompanied by, "Me love you long time!"

Watching this at home Catherine is thinking, *yep...grave condition indeed.*

Appalled media members, mortified White House staff, politicians uttering every oath and prayer, they all burst into action at the same time. Chaos takes control while everyone suddenly finds somebody in their way. The President tries to explain away the situation but words fail him. People are clamoring to turn off the system, to snap a picture, to get a quote, to get out of sight. Meanwhile, the United States becomes increasingly manic in its actions with China.

"Me love you long time! Me love you long time!"

"For God's sake, somebody turn that off!"

"Mr. President! What—"

"Not now, not now—"

"Me love you—"

Some poor intern, drenched with sweat by this point, simply yanks every wire going to the monitor, killing the image. The screen instantly goes black; even the power supply was pulled loose.

"—long time! Me love you long time!" On hearing the disembodied pillow talk of China continuing to haunt the press room the staffers really freak out; this defies logic.

Without warning the President cowers behind the podium while thrusting an ornate Hungarian crucifix into the air shouting, "Begone! Begone!"

On top of this the Vice Pressy is rushing in to put the kibosh on this wretched scene, only in his haste he didn't change out of his hospital gown and his IV is dragging on the floor behind him.

"Where's it coming from, where's it—"

"Mr. President—"

"Jeffries, grab the VP—"

"—time! Me love you long time! Me—"

"Begone! The power of Christ compels you! The power of Christ compels you!"

"Mr. President—"

"—love you long time!"

Finally a pair of Secret Service agents shout a brusque warning and shoot out the two speakers attached to the independent audio system, amid the screams of reporters who had only moments ago been laughing it up. The Secret Service agents? A man of African descent and a redheaded woman.

Yes, their actions were my doing; what should I do, sit idly by? That is not my style. Not entirely.

Backstage the regrouping effort is not an easy one. The advisors are in disarray. Billings guides a dazed Mr. President back to their befuddled mass, catching them in mid conversation. "Good God above, I hope the Vice President didn't mess up that ape heart..."

"What?" The President exclaims and stands back, incredulous. "What did you just say? Would you care to repeat that?"

Realizing that the monkey is out of the bag the advisors go silent, biting their lips and trying to come up with something fast.

"I believe," Billings says, "I believe they said the Vice President has an ape heart."

"That's not what we said! No one ever said that. This was not said."

"You told me he was in for a check up!" the President blurts. "Getting some kind of baboon heart implant is a hell of a lot more than just some check up!"

"What I want to know," the Press Secretary blurts, "I think the question which demands to be answered is what in the world happened out there?!"

"Don't look at me," Billings defensively states.

"Check up huh? He'll be going for check ups down at the National

Zoo from now on..."

"The CGI media for the conference was in your care, Billings, you remember that!"

"Hey now, wait a second—"

The group falls silent when the two Secret Service agents who saved the day join them. The man, Cornelius, is the first to speak. "Are you all right Mr. President? Is everyone here all right?" He is quiet, calm, yet his voice bellies enough of his inner resolve to steady the shaken lot.

One of the shadow advisors, at the end of his patience, says, "The question is not whether we are okay. The question is what about those people out there?"

"No casualties in the Press Corps sir," the woman replies, missing his point. Her short-cropped red hair and stern gaze are not nearly as striking as her forceful demeanor.

Cooler heads prevail and the two unfamiliar agents are introduced to the President by the White House Security Chief. The reserved Agent Cornelius and the determined Agent Norton, two names the public are sure to become familiar with, despite the fact that they are so new to the job. Soon the group is joined by other subordinates, by a sober Bethany, and people shift into small talk mode.

"I would personally like to extend my gratitude to the two agents who saved my hide out there," the President says, shaking hands with each.

Cornelius nods. "Just doing our jobs, sir."

"So what are you?" the President asks Norton while smoothing out his suit. "Some kind of dyke? Is that what they're calling them these days?"

After a hesitation she replies, "Don't ask, don't tell. Sir."

"I mean really," he continues to his advisors, oblivious to her response. "Lesbos? You can't say that, am I right? Listen, I've got nothing against the military muff-munchers. They can kill a sand nigger just as easy as the next broad. Hmm. Well guys? We got a protocol for this? A sodomite protocol?"

Billings clears his throat and says, rather embarrassed, "The term 'sodomite' refers to male homosexuals, Mr. President."

"Oh...oh right. Well I'll bet the ladies do that strap-on thing, you know? Isn't that right Norton?" he chuckles in his best effort to be chummy. "I mean, we're all 'guys' here, right?"

A couple of them rush to volunteer chuckles in support of their leader, to save face for him. A couple are so humiliated by their association to this man, this scene, that they just kind of check their watches or busy themselves with spontaneous grooming. Norton's jaw muscles are clenched as she struggles to maintain composure; nobody has even paid attention to Cornelius enough to notice him fuming over the "sand nigger" comment. Not to mention the look the First Daughter has in her eye when she regards Norton.

It is decided that they need to get back to their offices and launch a damage control campaign as quickly as possible. They brusquely say their good-byes or thank-yous, or watch-your-backs, and depart. Norton and Cornelius are dismissed, much to their relief, and Bethany is sent to Georgetown by her father with a crisp roll of fifty-dollar bills. Only Billings lingers with the President once the dust has settled. The problem is that, while he can understand much of what went wrong out there, one thing keeps tripping him up.

"If you don't mind my asking sir...not that I'm one of these atheist heathens, as you know, but, ah, what was that business with the...um, the cross?"

The President gravely turns to "his man" fully ready to divulge his terrible secret. "We've got a denizen problem here Billings. There are denizens dwelling here." Billings nods, understanding the correct usage of the word. "I mean it son. I'm serious. We've got denizens living in the White House, or not living, as the case may be."

"I..." his subordinate begins, unsure. "I think I understand. The message will be relayed through the appropriate channels and facilitating entities will interface, re: the issue at hand."

"Entities? We have entities on our side?" The President is truly astounded by the revelation.

"Why...why, yes sir, Mr. President. We have governmental entities at our disposal—"

"Do we now?"

"—yes sir, and there are law enforcement entities we can call upon, and even corporate entities in times of crisis."

"You don't say! Corporate entities?"

"Yes sir."

"Well now lick my balls and call me Charles! If that don't beat all. I do believe we have this denizen matter in the sack."

"I, ah, concur sir."

"Absolutely. That's great, that's great Big B. Good job I've got you around." The President stops to wipe his brow now, overcome by relief, and can't wait to tell his wife the good news. "I still can't get over that. Government entities? Is this a new development? Some breakthrough in the so-called science of the paranormal?"

Thoroughly confused now Billings says, "Not to the best of my knowledge sir, but I can look into the 'entity' thing if you so desire."

"No, no, that's quite all right. But you know what might hit the spot? If you can arrange to have the movie of the same title piped into the theatre tonight I'd appreciate that. It'll be a private viewing...if ya know what I mean."

"Um...sure thing...sir."

On that note I'll leave them be; even I have my limits.

$ $ $

The next time I check in on the situation another day has passed. Bethany mostly spent her time in Georgetown shoplifting and trying to ditch the people in the dark suits and sunglasses so she could score some narcotics, as if she needs to. Gordon has been up for over forty-eight hours in an unprecedented spring water binge. Catherine has been computing data and waiting patiently. The nation has been in a state of total outrage. China has been in a state of not only outrage but high alert. The President? He's going over some statistics he had requested from the last Census. Billings is conferring with him this very second.

"I've been looking over those statistics you gave me the other day. I've got to say, it's discouraging. I'm siding with Gibson on this one."

"Sir?"

"Just look at the numbers. We've got thirteen percent blacks, one percent Injuns, four percent Asians, twelve percent Spanish, ten percent gays...fifty-one percent women?! Holy God in heaven, this is our last stand! What's happened to the White Anglo-Saxon male?! Where is the White Anglo-Saxon male in all this?!"

"Sir—"

"Add up the numbers! Add 'em up, go on ahead. Ninety-four! Ninety-four! Do you know what that means?!?"

"Sir—"

"There's only six percent white men, good white God-fearing woman-loving men left in our country! This is our Alamo, a nation-wide Alamo!"

Billings almost mentions that the Alamo was fought by whites who wanted to own slaves in Mexican territory, and they got butchered because the Mexican government rightfully wouldn't allow slavery. Instead, he tries to focus on the fact that the President's addition makes no sense. "Actually, when we say percent sir, what we mean by that is an average based on the concept of one hundred being the sum of all factors considered. If you will, permit me to expose the, ah, fallacy in the mathematics you are using here and—"

"Hold it, hold it, come on kid. You're losing me here. It's all about the numbers. Add them up. One plus thirteen plus four plus twelve plus ten plus fifty-one."

"Actually that's only ninety-one, not ninety-four, but the truth of the matter is—"

"Whoa now! Hold those horses! Did you just say what I think you said? By gum that gives us an extra three percent white males. That gives us a leg up on the Asians and the Injuns but the gays are still on top of us. No! No, wait, that's not what I meant to—"

"Sir," Billings interrupts, unable to deal with this conversation. "I think the race issue is concerning everyone right now. Obviously the remarks of Senator Gibson and the slight mishap at the press conference yesterday brought the race issue to the forefront. This is a good thing. This gives us, and the nation as a whole, a platform for talks. Reasonable talks, moderation, touching bases and healing, everyone in a show of patriotic courage, moving forward and putting everything behind us. This is a prime opportunity, Mr. President, for both yourself and Senator Gibson. That is why I want to arrange the two of you meet and agree on steps to take toward reaching the goals I just outlined; meet in person that is. The general feeling is that it would be for the best." Actually the advisors got together this morning and told Billings he can convince the President to fix things or start looking for a job back in Wyoming.

"Huh. That sounds like a good idea. Sure thing, Billaroo. Me and Gibson, mono facing mono. Why don't you arrange that?"

"Great idea sir. I'll get on it ASAP." Billings heads off knowing that he will spend the remainder of his day attempting to make this thing work. There will be cancellations, there will be countless humiliating calls, but his objective is to focus on prioritizing.

In the meantime Bethany has gone out of town, requesting a change in the normal Secret Service escort: she wanted Norton to accompany her for the evening and, as usual, the First Daughter got exactly what she wanted—it didn't even involve smashing anything this time. The other First Child has made a commitment to water sports of every kind and spends his entire day at an aquatics center. When the facility closes for the evening security has to forcibly eject Gordon, but he does not mind as he is used to getting into such situations over water. Senator Gibson's office has pretty much given up on the press releases for the time being. Other than the terrifying classified happenings which I cannot disclose to you, the night ends with a whimper, just the way most people would prefer.

$ $ $

It is as lovely a morning right now as you can expect from this season. I wish I could be out there enjoying it but, as my occupation demands, I have to keep my mind on the business at hand. As it stands the business of our nation's leader is my business.

At the moment he is feeling rather confidant—okay, he's downright cocky—after his impromptu meeting with Catherine Jauquesjourstd. The Administration managed to slip her in before the meeting with Senator Gibson and, as far as he's concerned, his head did an admirable job under the circumstances. There was no briefing, no script, his skull had to hold presidential form of its own accord. Catherine, for her part, is satisfied/disturbed that her suspicions were verified. She leaves the White House with the conviction that she must hold a press conference as soon as possible.

High on his performance with the skull woman the President lets his people hustle him and bustle him about; he doesn't really care where because he is no longer paying attention. Today he has discovered that perhaps the most fulfilling pastime in Washington, D.C. is to break with the script and fly solo, to improvise like those jazz people. Which leads to the next situation. There was a strong push by both sides for their men to stick with a script for the duration of the meeting, but the politicians refused to have anything to do with that: this is an issue that can be settled as men in open and honest conversation.

This "face time" between the President and Gibson could be just what the doctor ordered, a shot in the arm to alleviate the nation's racial woes. The flipside is that it could be just what the junkie ordered and lead to an overdose which Billings—or anyone for that matter—will not be equipped to handle.

"Now Jefferson...Jeff...you mind if I call you Jeff?"

"Not at all Mr. President."

"Jeff." He hesitates just long enough to appear quite serious about what he is going to say. "We as leaders—as members of the same party—we as men or...as a man we need to, are needing as a man, has a need to resolve this issue for the betterment of the population of...the people, you know, the populace of constituents and those in the country who are non-constituated, we need to reach out to them too—I am a compassionate conservative after all—and accepting that view, that vision, of a broad-ranged spectrum all the way from the non-constituated to the constituated, embracing that view, championing that world view...well, not a 'world' view per se, but an American view, that is, we are talking about America after all...but with full commitment to this ideological mindset, mindframe, in mind, in hand—and I don't think you'll disagree with me here Fred—we are at a very dangerous stage in the development of the democratic, or, the ideal of democracy as we know it in America is at a dangerous place, the most dangerous since the Civil War and that whole civil rights thing, so the viewpoint in our mindset to the public needs to be one of holistic inclusivity for the masses, as a mass, or, as a person...as a person...no, caught myself there! I almost made a boo-boo. *To* a person, *to* a person, the American population needs to rest assured that they can put complete confidence in what we are representing for the present voters and the future voters, and the past voters too if they can get out of the nursing homes to the polling booths, as well as what we are representing to and for the future generations to come that have not been born yet, because that's something which is important, which people see as important, because it's the future and all that...people want something to invest in, not to investigate in, so we need as a man to make ourselves something not to be investigated in but invested in, to divest even, so when it comes to this whole...what I'm trying to say is that with the whole brouhaha lately blowing up in the media it could potentially be seen as giving the public a VPFAE to engage in a FCU ASAP leading to a SYA situation leading to a NKUE for you and me, and other members of the party. We need to be the example that the party sets, not the pity—or epitome, we can't be seen as the epitome, the disgrace if you will. Nobody's going to see us as pitiful. I'm nobody's epitome, I'm an example by gum!"

There is a silence, an utter silence, and Gibson looks to the side while wringing his hands. "I think I understand your gist Mr. President, understand it perfectly...and, in fact, I couldn't agree more!"

The President grins, pleased that such a complicated message was grasped by this man. He is so happy, in fact, that he gropes for a compliment to bestow on Gibson. "And might I add that your wife possesses exceptionalistic bosoms for her age, a perfect example of a woman who has aged gracefully to perfection, if you don't mind my saying so."

"Why...thank you, and might I compliment the First Lady on what couldn't be a finer posterior."

"Really? You think?"

"Absolutely." Then, wanting to clear things up a little, Gibson adds, "About the NKUE..."

"Yeah Fred? Fire away."

"Uh...yes, well, it could just be the neck of the woods that I inhabit, but I'm not familiar with that one."

"Non-Kosher Uncouth Ejection." They look to each other and laugh about this, both feeling that they've made a breakthrough in their relationship. "Tell you what," the President says, "I heard the big fight was going to be on today and arranged to have it available for you and me to watch, now how about that?"

"Sounds good to me. I think we have that other matter thoroughly settled anyhow."

"I think so." With one click of the remote control the President brings to life a seven-foot by ten-foot view of an arena in which the crowd is going haywire. Two heavyweights are in the process of beating each other into a prematurely decrepit state...in other words it is a great match.

"Look at that one there, in the red trunks," the President says in order differentiate between the two since they are both African American. "That one could be the black Mohammed Ali if you ask me." Gibson simply grunts, happy to be watching some good ol' fashioned knuckle dusting in progress, but this somehow reminds the President of another topic he wanted to discuss. "You know Senator, I wanted to ask you about something. When you made your recent comments was it after seeing the last census statistics? Because I have got to say that I took a gander at the numbers the other day and I was utterly horrified like you wouldn't believe..."

"You too? No lie my friend, no lie! What in the jumpin' jehosafats is going on? How can it be nobody else in the government is concerned about this?"

"That's what I wanted to talk about. There are others who, I feel, share the same opinions, are opinionated in the same vein, as you and I, on the matter of a need to take action. We have a plan and we'd like to have you on board, now that you've been set straight on the whole 'white-niggerism' thing, because what this all calls for is men of character that can carry out the plan without drawing too much attention to themselves in the process."

"Roger that."

"Glad to hear it."

"Ten four."

After a tete-a-tete of such magnitude both men need to replenish their reserves. The televised bout provides an easy-going diversion while it lasts and soon enough it is time to get back to the reality of running the world. The clock finally screams at them to get it in gear and they put their drinks down, exchange pleasantries which are forgotten as soon as they are spoken, and shake hands like men of honor.

On the way to the door the President turns to his man "Fred" for some closing remarks. "I'm glad you're a team player Fred. The team needs players. If it weren't for men such as you and myself we'd have monkeys running this place."

"I feel the same way Mr. President. I just hope that I'm able to help out."

"I have no doubts about that one. We're doing the good work. I am sure that you know well enough we are the superior race, scientifically speaking. As the president I'm living proof of that."

$ $ $

Not too far away, exactly twenty-four hours later, Catherine is beginning to address a gathering of reporters, having taken a devil-may-care attitude toward the discoveries that the White House held for her. “Good afternoon. My name is Catherine Jauquesjourstd. Most of you should be unfamiliar with the name but I am a specialist in the scientific field previously considered discredited, the field known as Phrenology.” This draws a solitary guffaw from the back of the crowd. “Go ahead and laugh, yes, Phrenology, or a crude variation of it, was basically used to discredit itself in the hands of totalitarian racists and hatemongers decades ago. What I have undertaken, though, is something that I believe you, the press, and the international scientific community at large—but more importantly the American people themselves—will find fascinating and horrifying in equal proportions.

“As this is no technical symposium, just an informal disclosure of findings, I shall attempt to relay everything in layman’s terms. But first, I offer a bit about my background, my credentials. My background lies not in work with humans, although I did train working with human subjects at a number of universities throughout North America and Europe. In addition I have continued to examine human skulls during my career when the opportunity has presented itself. My specialty, however, is in primate studies. I have worked at length with the bonobo or “pigmy chimp,” Pan paniscus, and the common chimpanzee, Pan troglodytes. There is quite a difference between the two, for those unfamiliar with chimps and bonobos. To put it simply the bonobo is physically smaller and much more intelligent, sometimes shockingly so, while the chimp possesses a more limited intellect. To the untrained eye, however, chimps and bonobos would appear the same. But this is not about the skulls of primates.

“I have been lucky enough to have the opportunity to enlist the participation of the First Family in an unprecedented scientific inquiry into the mind of a standing president. The cooperation of the

Administration in assisting my probe is to be commended; quite obviously many in positions of power would wish to have nothing to do with the field of phrenology. However, I will not delve today into the morphology of the the skulls of all the First Family members. While their cooperation is appreciated and their data helpful, the focus of my research is on the President himself."

She pauses to unveil the visual aides she has constructed. One details an enlargement of the President's head with the various measurements clearly marked. The other is of a chimpanzee with comparable measurements outlined. "As you can readily see for yourselves the President's skull clearly shares a majority of the characteristics exhibited in the skull of a chimp. Yes, a chimp, not a bonobo." She quells the uproar by raising her hands. "Please, please, I will take any and all questions very shortly. Now, there are several plausible explanations to be explored.

"There has been a long-standing theory regarding the extinction of the Neanderthals. The theory runs along the lines of possibilities involving the absorption of the Neanderthal into what we know as the modern homo sapien population. This is theoretically possible. When one summons the common image of Neanderthals it is not unusual to think of large, thick body types. We can point out large examples of modern humans so it stands to reason that relatively smaller or 'average'-looking Neanderthals could pass among us without notice. Is that what we have stumbled upon here?"

This causes what we in the government term an FCU—a Fucking Crazy Uproar—among the press. They frenzy instantly, the flashbulbs creating a shocking, nonstop ultra-noon while questions are shouted, yelled, snarled, literally thrown on scraps of paper or little paper airplanes. The physical crush of reporters maneuvering for position threatens to become a full-fledged riot. Lucky for Catherine

I have an interest in making sure she shares her findings with the world. It takes all of my effort, considering the number of people, but within seconds I have them reasonably calm, at least enough for them to realize that she has yet to finish with her presentation.

Catherine clears her throat. "I do concede that there are other explanations to be considered. Quite honestly I urge others to look at the alternate possibilities every bit as vigorously as the theory I proposed only moments ago. Casting aside the obviously preposterous notion that we have, in fact, discovered a proverbial 'missing link' between ourselves and the chimps the only other plausible explanation lies in the possibility of chromosomal damage, anomalies perhaps induced by radiation or the use of substances such as LSD during pregnancy. What is more likely though is the retrogressive effect of a chemical such as, God forbid, methyl-mercury, which would have to be introduced by the mother's body in high amounts during or just prior to insemination.

"Before we go any further I want to allow a few questions. Yes, you sir, in the tweed..."

"Yes, ah, you say your name is 'Hawkshurst.' How do you spell that? Just to keep us honest."

That might be another press conference all by itself, she's thinking.

$ $ $

Unfortunately something else has come up, a dire development, one that I have to turn my full attention to. The President is feeling the taxpayer oats at the moment, raising his bar, and a little bit nervous about it. At the same time it is a relief to have that squeaky-clean Billings kid out of the picture. The picture, at the moment, is a dark one indeed.

Agent Norton enters the chamber unaware of the situation. The President is sitting behind what would seem to be an ordinary desk, this is true, but the desktop itself is clear of anything you would find in a work space: there are no papers, no writing utensils, nothing. Aside from the two who brought Norton in, there are already a pair of Secret Service agents—men—waiting in the wings. One advisor or another is present, it really doesn't matter which. As for the contents of the desk, well, there are several types of lubricant available, many prophylactics, assorted "toys" and restraints, that sort of thing. Despite being a tad nervous the President forces a pleasant demeanor, with his hands folded on the desktop and that familiar election-winning smile being put to use.

"You wanted me sir?" Norton asks. It's true, she wonders about the dim lighting and lack of windows...in fact isn't this one of those "safe rooms" that is completely insulated from all forms of surveillance?

"Why, yes Norton, you could say that." He clears his throat, still uncomfortable. "Say, ah, why don't you have a seat there Norton." He gestures to the area directly in front of the desk despite the fact that no chairs are present. Within seconds one of the men has provided Norton with a chair and she sits. From what the President has been told this is how it's done around here, it's okay, *everything is complimentary...you're the President now.* "I'm not sure if you recall that conversation we had the other day, you know, things were a little topsy-turvey there and you came to the rescue, guns blazin' and all."

"Yes sir, that would be hard to forget."

Again he's clearing his throat. "Yes, well now, I suppose so." Two of the men have positioned themselves a couple feet behind her now; she seems to find this a bit peculiar but does not read anything sinister into it. "That was quite a ruckus there, eh? Norton? What's your first name by the way? I don't recall."

"Kendra, sir."

"Right, right. Well then Kendra...or do you go by Kenny? If you prefer I can roll with that. We can roll with that right gentlemen?"

"No, no sir, that's quite all right," she says while trying hard not to come off as perturbed.

"Kendra Norton. Norton Kendra. Well now, you ever get confused having two first names?" He slaps the desk now and a couple of the others laugh to break the tension...Norton even throws in a chuckle in the attempt to keep things running smoothly. *Everything is complimentary here.* "Well the thing is..." *This is the way it's done sir*, they had assured him. The wife and kids have been escorted to some charity event, God knows where, so what is he worried about? "I'm sure you're familiar with our Coalition of the Willing, and how important it is to the security of our fine nation. The focus here is on the 'willing' part of it."

"I'm not sure I understand, sir." Norton has a dinner date and hopes this won't take very long. She'd like to get home, spruce up, feed her birds, etc., before then.

Gingerly tapping his fingers together the President looks to his men—who aren't sure if they should take this as "the signal"—and to his advisor, who sort of makes a "hurry up" gesture. "The thing is, Norton, Kendra, Kendra Norton if you will, but I guess nobody really calls you that, all at once like that I mean...well, you know, the thing is that you never really answered my question the other day."

In the silence that falls over the room Norton is starting to feel a little lost. What's it all about? Why leave her equipment behind? What stupid question the other day? All she remembers is the overwhelmingly ignorant impression he had made on her. "I...would you please clarify sir?"

"That whole strap-on thing. You know what I'm talking about. Right?"

There is a tense silence and the surprising embarrassment causes her to giggle slightly. "You can't be serious..."

"You know Norton, Kendra, there's been some discontent among the staff, I mean with your lifestyle and all."

"Sir, I've made no statement regarding any lifestyle that I might lead–"

"And there have been rumors, unkind rumors, rumors circulating around here about you making, well how can I say this other than to say it, but inappropriate comments and gestures and such, inappropriate contact, with a member of my family–"

"Mr. President, that is completely unfounded–"

"Let me finish. As I was saying, the word I hear is that you have alledgedly had inappropriate contact with my daughter. Now that is a serious accusation."

Norton is thinking, *as if*. That brat made her moves, insisting they eat at a fancy restaurant, go to a movie, grab some desert, then got a bit too personal and it went no further than that; Norton found the entire "assignment" to be tasteless and demeaning. "So are you trying to say you want me removed from White House duty? You're going to reprimand me? Maybe fire me outright...is that it?"

"No, no, not at all. I think everyone here will agree to your competency. No. What I'm saying is that I'd like an in-depth answer to my question, if you will." She has no response to this so he places one of the devices from the drawer on the desk top. "Maybe...maybe a demonstration would be the best thing. What do you think?"

"What do I think? What do I think? I'll tell you what I think–"

"I'll level with you Norton. That stunt the other day, when you came barging in blasting bullets in a room full of civilians like it was World War III, well, I'm afraid that's caused quite an FCU as they say. You're in some hot water here little lady. But never let it be said that we don't protect our own, we do. I don't see any need for criminal misconduct charges to be leveled against you. That other one, Cornelius, he's been dealt with already. I think it's in your best interest to cooperate."

More aware than ever that her weapons are not with her Norton judges the men from the corners of her eyes, trying to decide what chance she has of striking some pressure points and simultaneously bolting for the door. Well, there are four of them, each trained as well as her presumably. The distance across the desk? She could easily get hold of the President, perhaps...no, they could just shoot her, at that range from four different angles one should have a clear shot even if the President was used as a shield. The only choice is to disarm one of them, hold the weapon on President to get out of there...and then? Who cares.

This is bad, even worse than I expected. I'd better create some kind of diversion, something that will interrupt the goings on at the highest levels of our government. Even so, I should still be able to concentrate on what's happening in that room, to hear and see their actions.

Two of the men are wrestling with Norton now, and the sudden violence causes the President to jump from his seat. In the shadows the advisor is yawning. The others are fingering their guns. Using the mechanics of the wrist and shoulder joints against her the men manage to pin Norton to the desk. The stream of curses from her mouth earns her a blow to the back that steals her breath. This is all a bit too extreme for the President. None of this is going the way he had envisioned. From the shadows the advisor finally catches his eye, urging him to get on with it. The men are watching him, waiting for their leader to take the actions expected of him. Well, he promised that he would go to Washington and get things done. Finally he has to lead by example and take some action, come what may, so he walks around the desk as coolly as he can under the circumstances. And standing behind Norton, admiring the view looking down on her, what does he see exactly? The fabric of Norton's dark suit stretched taught across her curves, form-fitting like black oil smeared over vulnerable flesh.

Billings bursts into the room, all bluster and *gosh oh man* and *this is the end* with his deodorant failing him already, his sleeves rolled up like when he used to help his father with the wood carving, and *aw shucks* he's got to tell them, he's got to begin damage control. "Mr. President sir, we—" and then he comes to a halt, all the guards turning to him, some with a hand on their weapon, and Norton pinned to the desktop...suddenly things are actually worse than Billings realized; the coalition of the willing has become the coalition of the drilling.

The President faces Billings with hands in pockets, looking like he's been caught with his hand in the cookie jar. "I don't guess your mother ever told you to knock first?" he says as if joking. "That's a pretty important lesson there. All my kids know to knock before coming into a room." He casually saunters back behind the desk and plops down in the cushy chair, resting his feet on the desktop. "Well, you're here, now aren't you? Guess we're open for business then. Fire away bucko." Unsure of what the situation demands of them the men release Norton on a silent command from the advisor in the shadows. They are all standing in silence—well the leader is sitting—just sort of staring uneasily at the walls or the floor or the desk, Norton with the blood flushing her face and the fear jittery in her eyes. The President laughs uneasily because he's not capable of anything else. "Well? Commie got your tongue? Spit it out now."

Billings wants to just turn and walk away now, let everything blind-side the leader of the free world, but he knows somewhere inside of him that the truth of the situation is this man will find out in a matter of minutes, maybe seconds, regardless. "Sir, there's been an accident." After a gulp he adds, "Your family sir." Something changes in the room now and those words bear down on everyone like a Russian sickle and hammer. "The helicopter sir." He won't bother mentioning the chimpanzee thing until later. "I'll be back in the Coordination Room, uh, coordinating."

"You do that..." The President is too stricken at this point to care what Billings does.

"Why don't I escort you," Norton says, grabbing Billings by the arm. "You never know what can happen during an emergency situation." She drags him through the door and the others look to the shadow advisor, but he shakes his head in the negative. Norton and Billings are safe. For now.

$ $ $

The day after a traumatic experience is always the worst. You no longer have the adrenaline rush, the blinding emotions, just the sober realizations and riddles that life leaves scrawled in the ashes.

"We are all very thankful that nobody was severely injured, Mr. President." The Vice President is briefing the leader of the free world on the accident. He has pretty much been running the show—officially since last evening, due the to President's all-night vigil at the hospital—and this is the first chance he and the President have had to discuss matters in private. "Helicopter kicked up a fair amount of dirt on impact but no bystanders were injured. Also, nobody knows that the pilot was letting Gordon fly the copter when the incident occurred. That is, only the pilot and your family, but I have the feeling the pilot's condition may take a turn for the worse...if need be."

The President is solemnly staring out the window, observing the lawn of the executive mansion. "What was his Aqua-Aqua intake for the day?"

The Vice President hesitates. "Nine-point-three gallons."

"My God..." the President marvels.

"Mr. President, I think there is a little information that you should be privy to. Our sources inform us that Aqua-Aqua is not pure spring water. It does contain additives...habit-forming additives."

"Habit-forming," the President repeats, the meaning slowly sinking in. How is it his second in command always knows more than he does? "So...they're even putting stuff in the water to keep you hooked. It's okay, we'll blame it on one communist conspiracy or another."

"You're getting the hang of this sir." There is a thoughtful pause. "About that other thing, well, I wouldn't lose too much sleep over it."

"Oh? You wouldn't? They're trying to impeach me for *not being a human*, for the love of–"

"It's all unfounded Mr. President. There would have to be an exhaustive inquiry into the matter by a team of scientists who were approved by both liberals and conservatives in Congress. That alone will probably eat up another year or two. Then we could stonewall the thing well into the next administration. Nothing will come of any of this."

"Listen, Vice-Pressy, if I wasn't human you'd tell me, right?"

"Of course sir, of course." He realizes the President is waiting expectantly so he adds, "There can be no doubt as to whether or not you are a human being sir."

"If that's the truth then why are they marching in the streets?! Why are they chanting 'Boo, boo, put him in the zoo!' Answer me that. What do they want from me anyway? Is it a scheme to get another three big ones? Because I'll tell you what, the treasury can handle that much buster, yessiree Bob, but I won't dole out any more of the pie. Nada. Because it's extortion is why! Dag-blammit, you give 'em an inch and they'll take a mile." Silence intervenes and soon enough the tension eases out of the President. "Is there anything else going on I should know about?"

The Vice President checks his fingernails. "The EPA needs to relax about the arsenic levels found in the public drinking water around mining operations. It's perfectly healthy. You know, back in Victorian times, arsenic was the equivalent of an over-the-counter-drug that was widely administered for a number of purposes. Arsenic has truly been maligned by all these fiction writers and muckrakers just because people can overdose on the stuff. Well, I'll say! A person can overdose on caffeine, can't they?"

"Wow...I never thought about it like that..."

"Now you have the correct view on the issue, Mr. President. Another matter of significance is that people are putting our performance over hot coals just because employment has dropped to four-year lows in all business sectors. What these pundits fail to mention is the fact that twenty-two thousand new jobs have been created in the oil and coal industries!"

"As it should be, as it should be. Beaucoup...beaucoup..."

Red flags go up for the Vice President. He makes a mental note to have the President examined and then...yes, yes, perhaps a six-week vacation is in order. After all the stress the man has been through recently he shouldn't be expected to continue performing. Despite the fact that he is the headliner the show can go on without him. In fact the show may actually prosper from his absence.

Nobody has seen or heard from Kendra Norton.

Catherine Jauquesjourstd is on a plane bound for France. The death threats came pouring in almost immediately, as well as the wrath of the scientific community. To the best of her estimates her efforts were a success: she highlighted a troubling fact while also bringing phrenology to the fore. Nobody is likely to forget either of these things for quite some time. The hope is that the European community will not make as harsh an assessment of her actions.

That leaves only one other loose end...the man who barged in on our leader when his arm was in the cookie jar up to his shoulder. The man who knew the President's every move, every thought. The idealistic young guy from out west who did not make enough friends in the Administration. The guy stepping into his own home and finding an ominous man sitting in the living room. Seeing the large man in the dark suit and sunglasses gives Billings the feeling that he is in grave condition now. This is what we call a Damage Control Operative. You won't find DCO's mentioned in the PR pamphlets, that's for sure. They are yet another non-existent extension of the government.

"Mr. Billings. The Administration wanted me to stop by and talk to you about the termination of your position at the White House. Please, make yourself comfortable. Have a seat." The DCO gestures to a chair directly across from him.

His termination? Billings does as he is told, cautiously, trying to remember a prayer—any prayer—and failing.

The man opens a briefcase and angles it in toward Billings. Inside is the largest sum of money that he has ever seen. "We do believe that you will find the severance package to be satisfactory. In addition to the severance package we realize that a young man such as yourself, with your talents and political prospects, is too valuable to cut loose entirely. To this end we have performed a search of job openings at your current salary within the federal government. The first thing to pop up was a survey that needs to be conducted in Tahiti. The assignment lasts four years and all expenses are paid for. We believe certain key elements in your experience make you the perfect candidate for the job."

Billings' head is swirling now. In short the world has just dropped out from under his feet. "I...I don't know what to say..."

"Say yes."

"Say...yes?"

"Excellent, we are most pleased that you have accepted the position.

Here are your tickets, along with all pertinent information regarding the assignment." The man places a manila envelope in one of Billings' hands and the briefcase in the other. He does not need to tell Billings that the position was created to get him out of the District of Columbia.

"I...I accepted, huh? Well. I guess, uh, thanks." Billings sort of grins because he doesn't know what else to do. "And if I hadn't, you know, 'accepted' the position?"

The man stares at Billings long enough for the awkward grin to drain from his features. "Let me just repeat the we are most pleased that you have accepted the position." He stands. "We don't have any time. I am to escort you to the airport and another man will accompany you to your destination. He will fill in any blanks regarding the job. All belongings you wish to have shipped to you in Tahiti will be taken care of at the Administration's expense."

Billings considers the mind-boggling amount of cash in his possession and the dream job he has been thrust into. *Everything is complimentary here.*

Sometimes I'm shocked that these people aren't all bruised from the system's udders slapping them in the face year-round. The way they milk the system, it's frightening. Then again what can I say? I took the big payoff and pension plan and everything else.

Oh? What *about* me, you ask? I'm the White House Pyschic-Ops agent. That's right, I'm part of the Psychic Operations unit that is an extension of the paranormal division which officially does not exist in our government. And about that bogus tax return my friend, well, somebody will be visiting you soon enough...any minute now. Why else would I keep you preoccupied with this pathetic tale?

Deface the Nation

"A PROSTITUTE WAS ARRESTED earlier today for *slap*ping a congressman with, of all things, a *dead fish*. This occurred after an incident in which the woman *claims* the senator *laughed* at her from the window of his limousine, which was parked on 9th street in Southwest D.C. earlier this after*noon*. The senator, Democrat *Richmond Hale* of *Nebraska*, has refused to comment on the incident. His staff did issue a statement, however, assuring the public that doctors have concluded Senator Hale is free of food poisoning. The alleged fish had not been properly re*frigerated* prior to the attack."

Damn, damn, double damn! The TelePrompTer said "fish alledgedly" not "alleged fish" for Christ's sake. What do they want from me anyhow? I can't be expected to glean anything intelligible from that obsolete piece of crap. "In other news the police in Woodly, Virginia have made an *arrest* in the *case* of a college coed who was *sexually assaulted* earlier this week by a member of the Woodly Lights Shopping Mall *security*. *Leonard Little*, thirty-eight, of nearby *Grammercy*, Virginia, has a criminal record with two convictions for violent offenses. The victim's family is understandably *out*raged." Yeah, yeah, Marty, I know we're running a clip of the dumb bitch's father acting pissed off so their law suit can suck more money from the mall. Like I haven't been doing this my whole adult life? Good

God above, between this and the libral slant of these stories, I have to get this guy fired. At least the security footage of the attack should pull some strong numbers.

Yes, damn it all, I know we're back on in three, two, one, "The attack occurred during the small scale riot which broke out due to left-wing extremists at one of the mall's book stores. It so happened that famous counter-culture author William Pollock experienced a nervous breakdown that instigated these events, due to years of drug abuse. Pollock, a well-known pillar of the *liberal media conspiracy*, is now convalescing at the *Fontworth* Center in Indiana. The recent pub*licity* has spurred flagging book sales on to the greatest success he's had in *years*, resurr*ecting* an otherwise *dead* career. If you are interested in finding out more about Pollock's works you can *log on* to the *inter*net at CopyrightExtorters.com." Damn, it didn't used to be this way, shucking and jiving to move merchandise. I should have been the next Cronkite! I'm stuck in this damned swamp? I don't care if it is the most important city in the world...oh my Lord, if I have to listen to Jane's voice for even one more second I'm going to have an aneurism, I swear! Who knows what she's saying, and who cares.

Thank the Almighty for commercial breaks. I'll spend this one meditating I think...yes...hmm...revenge...ah...well, that was quick. "The *financial front* is not looking good this evening." Financial front? "Reports of a *sliding national economy* are fueling concerns about a repeat of the economic slumps experienced in the *1930's* and *1980's*. There is no indication that such will be the case, in fact all signs are pointing to a *rebound* now that the President's tax refund plan has gone into effect. The troubles on Wall Street were started by the *announcement* last week that the *Federal surplus* has dropped by *nearly* eighty percent. A congressional inquiry is scheduled to look into the matter."

My lovely—if you can call a mannequin with make-up lovely—co-anchor turns to me. "I wonder how the people feel about that Mike?"

"Let's go to the man in the street and find out, Jane." I know my smile looks sincere enough as they cut away to the footage of our roving "man in the street" crew.

From the appearance of the man on the monitor, all gray and scraggly with pedestrians moving in the background, they've found themselves a guy just one step above a hobo. "Where'd the money go? There was a budget surplus, sure. You ask me—and I guess ya did—but it's sorta obvious what happened. Yeah. The democrats pocketed it all before they left office." I'll have to commend Jeremy on digging up such a dirty old rascal, an impoverished-looking type, to lend credence to what we need him to say. What I wonder, though, is why pay this schmuck fifty bucks when my speaking style is so much more dramatic?

This is followed by a clip of that Jirina phone psychic hussey spouting her nonsense, with some voiceover about how her dire predictions agitated the climate of fear on Wall Street. "I see him! It is clear...the Almighty! He is in pain, we have—*pain* I say—we have caused this, somehow. He doubles over, yes, oh yes, and in the heavens above us he squats...there is a final convulsion and...something is *falling!* It is dropping down on our *heads!* It is...*no!* It is the President!" Rumor on the D.C. streets is the First Couple stiffed Jirina on a check.

Jane does her fashion-shoot smile and says, "In other news the FBI has issued a warning to citizens to be on the lookout for a pair of bankrobbers. The two suspects are responsible for at least three armed robberies in the south, from North Carolina to Missouri, and are considered extremely dangerous. They have killed four bank employees and injured over a dozen bystanders during their crimes so we strongly urge viewers not to approach the suspects."

"Yes Jane. We ask that you simply call the number appearing on the screen if you see either of these persons."

The first mug shot is of an androgynous sort with dark hair and circles under their eyes. For some bizarre reason the following mug shot is of...a heart? I'll get whoever is behind this one, I swear. I am Mike-by-God-Radley and I won't have this any more!

Maurice hops in with a traffic report featuring a close-up through the windows of a nudist tour bus broken down on the beltway. Ramona tap dances through the weather and I can only wonder: why? Jane is already practicing her somber face before the cameras are back on us.

"This evening we have a sad story to report," that bimbo intones. Damn! This is the good stuff; it should be me doing this story, not her. The producers are convinced tragic stories come off more emotional when a dame does the talking. "In a sad ending to a story we have all been following for days now, the body of Josephine Baker Baxter *was* discovered today after a week-long search for the girl. The Baxter family and their community were heartbroken." Enough of this footage of people crying and blubbering and whatnot. Don't the producers realize the only way to use blacks on camera is to have them singing or cracking jokes? It's a proven fact. "Josephine Baxter was only six years old at the time of her death," the ditz continues. "She apparently became trapped after playing in an old refrigerator that had been left outside by the home's previous owners. Officials strongly urge all families to identify and remove any refrigerators or freezers which do not comply with current safety standards. Also, you are advised to screen your child's play area for any safety risks including old appliances, rusting metal, sinkholes, and glass objects."

"*Sinkholes*, Jane?" I can't help it. They've pushed me too far.

No, she can't find any of this in her notes or on the TelePrompTer. "Yes, that is one of the many safety risks which families are advised to watch for."

"That's right folks. You don't want your child to get a sprained ankle." The floor director is having a fit so I add, "Nearly three-hundred children suffer crippling sprains each year in the United States. In fact we have set up a fund here at the station if you care to make a donation for the children during this time of heightened safety awareness. Jane, would you be kind enough to give us that information?"

"Why...of course, Mike." Long pause. "Concerned citizens are urged to send their donations to the...Save An Ankle Foundation, care of Liberty Broadcasting Network, 2549 Annabelle Street North West, Washington, D.C. 20083." Jane's face is a flattering shade of crimson as we switch to a close-up of the *Hardline Nation* logo.

This is my favorite part. "Don't go away ladies and gentlemen, we will be *right back* with another *edition* of *Hardline Nation.*" And...fade to commercials.

"All right Radley, you dripping fuckhole, I've had it with your fucking bullshit! You fall in line or you're out the door!" That idiot floor director goes through this every time, for the sake of the others, because even if I call my own shots he doesn't want the rest to get any bright ideas. "You hear me?"

"Yeah, yeah, you know where you can go."

"Don't get bitchy! Don't get bitchy with me! You hear?"

My only reply is to laugh and sip some coffee. "Oh dear. You haven't forgotten the students from Pinewood Elementary here to see how the news is made, have you Marty?"

That idiot's face when he turns and sees the children, oh it's too much. Unfortunately that air-head Jane kicks me under the desk and ruins the moment. It takes the rest of the commercial break to get myself settled in over at the *Hardline Nation* set. By the time we are ready to go live again I'm just realizing that the one guest is sitting only a few feet away. I was so preoccupied with thoughts about the man who will join us via satellite that this other chump slipped my mind.

Soon enough the theme music is fading in, fading out, and it's my time to shine once more. "*Good evening* and welcome to another edition of *Hardline Nation*. Obviously the top news of the day, the tragedy that has occurred in the Midwest, will be discussed tonight, and we will have a guest who will provide *insightful commentary* on the subject. But before I go any further let me say that it is both my *privilege* and *pleasure* this evening to be able to introduce to our *viewing audience* two gentlemen who are easily among the most distinguished Americans, in fact among the *most distinguished* men worldwide, internationally, in the fields of the arts and politics." Who the hell is writing this tripe? "Firstly I welcome, here in the studio with us tonight, the winner of the Nobel Prize in literature...Mr. *Willard Pretorious*."

"Why thank you for having me, Mr. Radley. As always it is an honor to share my thoughts in a public forum."

Whatever. "And next, ladies and gentlemen, I would like to introduce a man who today had to make two of the most difficult phone calls of his life...the *President of the United States of America*. It is an honor sir."

The President's image comes in live via satellite on a huge monitor stationed next to Pretorious. "Thank you Mikey. I appreciate the kind words, but first I would like to address the incident you just brought up."

"By all means, Mr. President. It must be extremely difficult losing two of the people sworn to protect your life."

"No truer words have been spoken Mikey. To the families and the loved ones of the deceased I would like to personally, as President of the United States of America, offer my sincere apol—*condolences*, condolences, I would like to offer my most sincere condolences on this solemn night." This is sure to boost the ratings. When a helicopter goes down under mysterious circumstances in the middle of nowhere carrying two Secret Service agents, and you're able to scoop the President himself...that's just money in the bank, plain and simple.

"Have the names of the deceased been released Mr. President?"

"No, Mikey, not as far as...no. We can say that one was a male and one was a female."

"Is there a *fear*, Mr. President, a *fear* that this may have been a miscalculated attempt on your life? That somehow persons of dubious intent thought you would be aboard the helicopter?"

"No, not at all Mikey, that's one thing I will say loud and clear this evening. There is no evidence of foul play at this time."

"Now, is it possible, Mr. President, that this could have anything to do with the relatively minor helicopter crash involving the First Family only a *short time*—" My question is interrupted by the giggles of none other than our leader.

"I'm sorry, please," the President says, clearing his throat. "Please excuse me."

Pretorious scowls. "Whatever do you find amusing in this subject matter, Mr. President?"

"Nothing, nothng at all. It's just, well I think I speak for all of us—I was, after all, elected to represent the public by the overwhelming mandate of the people—when I say that I'm glad you got yourself a new toupee."

There is a moment of silence. As hard as it is to believe the President really is this crass—or, as his supporters prefer to phrase it, *he has balls*.

"Quite a bit of bravado, is it not, coming from the dregs of the Stone Ages," Pretorious quips.

"Hey! Nothing's been proven about that!"

"*Quite so*, Mr. President," I say in the hopes of moving things along.

"That lady's a quack! Everyone knows it. Come on Mikey, fire away, I'm ready for any question you can throw my way. 'Bring it' as they say."

Before I can speak Pretorious jumps in with, "It is my understanding, Mr. Radley, that apes beat their chests when they get frustrated, which results from a profound lack of intellect. That's what separates man from beast my friend, the indelible, the sublime gift of intellect."

"Thanks for that illuminating bit of information, Mr. Pretorious," I say. "I'm sure our viewers appreciate it. Now Mr. President I'd like to bring to the fore a *subject* which has been lost in all the sensational reporting lately. That is the *Global Warming Initiative Treaty*. I understand this has been a source of some criticism for your administration, Mr. President—"

"'Some' criticism..." Pretorious snickers.

"What's that?" the President asks, semi-amused in his anger. "What's that? Got something to say? Come on out and say it."

Pretorious snickers again and I say, "Gentlemen—"

"Come on," the President urges. "Speak up there smarty-pants. Why don't you just spit it out? Or maybe—"

"Oh, I've more than enough to say on the matter, my conservative friend—"

"I sincerely doubt that I'm you're friend, pal."

"Touché. This treaty, like many other subjects, is a thing that I feel does nothing but condemn you sir, if not in the eyes of the citizenry of the United States then in the eyes of the rest of the world, mine included."

"Is that why you were wearing that ridiculous wig when you got your award? You couldn't see straight?"

"You are impossible, honestly, I've never seen anything like this from a politician. Not even during the tumult which swept the nation during my youth—"

The President slaps his knee and laughs. "Why, I'll bet back in the 1960's and 70's you were hugging trees like a dog humping its master's leg!"

"Why, of all the insufferably crude—"

The President interrupts with what I can't help viewing as an althogether childish burst of laughter. "Pretorious huh? Why, they ought to call you Pretentious...Willard Pretentious!"

Pretorious' face sinks to new shades of red as he slowly speaks. "You, sir, are in and of yourself validation for my move to Sweden, and may God take pity on those who have been left behind in the abstrusified zone designated as the United States of America."

I make the attempt to interject a comment but the President bulls through with, "Oh yeah? The same to you pal."

"There!" Pretorious exclaims, pointing harshly at the monitor. "There! You see?! That comment makes no sense! None at all! The same to me?! How on Earth can that comment be turned on me? You feel sorry for every United States citizen because they remain here, while you yourself moved to Sweden?!"

"Why not!" the President erupts.

"But—" Pretorious begins, shaking a fist madly, prepared to launch into an epic tirade before I cut him off.

"I am sorry, sirs, but I do believe we have gotten off the topic at hand here a bit—"

"Well don't look at me! He started it," the President says while adjusting himself in his seat in a vain attempt to find a comfortable position.

"Oh! Oh! And should we now degenerate to name calling and finger pointing?!"

"You already pointed your finger at me, or my monitor me, the 'big-screen me' if you will, so cast the first stone at yourself pal and get out of that glass house before it turns into cards...a house of cards that is, glass cards, you're getting stoned in a glass house. Of cards." The President has made his first decisive, valid point of the night, although it was so mangled in its delivery that I doubt it did him any good.

Pretorious cranes around in his seat to stare at me in confusion, his profound perplexity readily apparent and most likely exaggerated in an attempt to take full advantage of the President's convoluted verbiage. "My word. I do believe we have confirmation of Dr. Jauquesjourstd's allegations. Have you the number of the zoo Mr. Radley?"

"Oh yeah, well, that's sure clever enough," the President retorts, smashing his fist on the arm of his chair. "No wonder you're the big man in the book world."

"I am afraid gentlemen that we'll have to hold that thought. Don't go away...*Hardline Nation* will be right back after this brief message from our sponsors." The three of us refuse to speak to each other, or even look at each other, during the break. Marty and I aren't communicating directly either. When we come back the producers have me drop the question routine; obviously we won't get anywhere with that when it comes to these two buffoons.

"Let's open up the phone lines to calls from all over the country, calls from concerned citizens who have inquiries about the burning issues of the day for our two most esteemed guests." They're just doing this to embarrass me, those TelePrompTer assholes, I know our copywriters and the editor are not this inept. "Hello, Brody in Chantaloona? This is Mike Radley of *Hardline Nation*. I understand you have a question for the president of the United States of America. He is with us right now so please speak your piece." Speak your piece?! Speak your piece?! How many of these jerks have been smoking their pieces?! All of them, I'd wager. This has just been an all-around attrocious evening. Now they want me to sound like some sort of down-home bumpkin I suppose.

"Hello? Uh...hello?"

Christ, not another one of these people. "Yes, you are live on the air with Nobel laureate Willard Pretorious and the President of the United States. Do you have a question sir?"

"Yeah, yeah...my name is Brody and I live in Chantaloona. You know Chantaloona? It's where th' dance come from. Called the Chantaloona Hell-Hell? Ever heard of it?"

"Let's go to the next caller," I say, killing the line.

"Hey! What happened just there? My other phone line went dead. Good thing I called on all my lines. So anyway, like I was saying, I'm in the penitentiary here in Chantaloona and I wanted to comment to the President about the money situation."

"Do I have to take this call Mikey? Obviously this guy's a crackpot and doesn't have anything worth saying, so..."

"Mr. President!" Pretorious admonishes.

"What was that? *What was that?*" the man on the phone says. There is an uncomfortable silence in which nobody speaks. "Was that...was that the President talking?"

"Why yes it was, good sir!" Pretorious offers.

"Well then Mr. President. What I got to say is simple. One day...you'll get an envelope in the mail. And in that envelope you will find a piece of paper, mark my words. And on that slip of paper will be an I.O.U., yeah, that's right, an I.O.U. for the amount of $517.46 mister—"

The President blurts, "Okay, I think we've heard enough out of you punk—"

"*I owe you $517.46! Don't you forget it!*"

"I apologize to everyone involved but I'm afraid *that* is quite enough of *that*," I'm saying, enjoying the fact that I am once again the full-fledged moderator and no longer an observer. "Before we move on to the next caller though I would like to ask something—"

"Actually, first Mr. Radley, I would like to ask our intrepid leader something in order to clarify a point." That son-of-a-bitching Pretorious! "How is it the oil interests can put millions of dollars in your wallet but you're still sweating a measly debt of five—"

"Oh, put a sock in it Preposterous, or whatever your name is."

"It is no wonder that the United States is quickly losing the substantial budget surplus left by the previous administration. You're a rich kid and a dilettant, a rich kid who never had to cover his own debts, so how in creation can you be expected to balance the collective check book of a nation three-hundred-million strong?"

"That's it," the President huffs. "You stay right there. I'm coming down."

Pretorious gushes, "'Again I hear the creaking step! He's rapping at the door! Too well I know the boding sound that ushers in a bore.' The words of John Godfrey Saxe, although I doubt you've any familiarity with *My Familiar*."

While Pretorious is laughing the President is cracking his knuckles. "I'll meet you in five minutes buddy."

Oh no he doesn't! "Wait, Mr. President—" Damn! He's already flung off his clip-on mic and stormed off! The live satellite feed is of an empty chair. The producers are all screaming different things in my ear and the children in the studio are chanting "*Fight! Fight! Fight!*" and that Pretorious fool is laughing and shaking his head and Marty is about to go into convulsions. Not knowing what to say I clear my throat. "Well, ladies and gentlemen, that wraps up another edition of *Hardline Nation*. Please join us tomorrow, and, ah, back to you Jane."

"To sum it up," Pretorious says with flair, "'Among the blind the one-eyed is a king.' I bid you farewell!" He strikes a clever pose, dons a fake smile, and at long last we fade to black.

About the Author

John Edward Lawson is an author, editor, and publisher living just outside Washington, DC. He is co-writer and producer of *Rage: Internal Demons*, set for shooting in January 2008. A number of his poems have been adapted to film by renegade filmmaker Royce Icon. Lawson's poetry collections include *The Troublesome Amputee*, *The Plague Factory*, *The Horrible*, and *The Scars Are Complimentary*. Fiction includes *Last Burn in Hell*, *Pocket Full of Loose Razorblades*, and *Some Harm, Mostly Foul*. While serving as editor-in-chief of Raw Dog Screaming Press and *The Dream People* webzine, John has also been editor of the anthologies *Tempting Disaster*, *Sick*, and *Of Flesh and Hunger*. In 2001 he was a winner of the Fiction International Emerging Writers competition; award nominations include the Bram Stoker Award, the Rhysling Award, and the Pushcart Prize. Spy on him at www.johnlawson.org.